WHISPERS UNDER THE WHARF

Whispers Under the Wharf

A Monterey Ghost Story

by
VINCENT DIGIROLAMO
illustrated by BRUCE ARISS

FITHIAN PRESS   SANTA BARBARA   1990

"Sardine Fleet" painting by Bruce Ariss
© 1984 Monterey Bay Aquarium, photograph by Geoffry Johnson.
Cover design by Ric Masten.

Published by Fithian Press
Post Office Box 1525
Santa Barbara, California 93102

9 8 7 6 5 4 3 2

LIBRARY OF CONGRESS CATALOGING-IN-PUBLICATION DATA
DiGirolamo, Vincent
    Whispers under the wharf / Vincent DiGirolamo.
        p.   cm.
    Summary: Two brothers, one living and one a ghost, have
an adventure in the waterfront community of Monterey, Cali-
fornia, in the 1950s.
    ISBN 0-931832-52-7: $8.95
    1. Ghosts—Fiction.   2. Monterey (Calif.)—Fiction.
        I. Title.
PZ7.D57655wh 1990
[Fic]-dc20
                                            90-30173
                                              CIP
                                              AC

TABLE OF CONTENTS

Jenko's Prologue ... 7

1. The Secret Shed ... 9
2. The Skiff's Rescue ... 20
3. The Unveiling ... 34
4. Marooned ... 50
5. Whispers Under the Wharf ... 64
6. Gao's Curse ... 79
7. Spook On the Loose ... 90
8. A Death Defied ... 104
9. A Grave Encounter ... 118
10. Moonseeker ... 129
11. Red's Return ... 137
12. Halloween Horrors ... 143
13. Maiden Voyage ... 153
14. Discovery ... 164

Jenko's Epilogue ... 172

For all my family

He ne'er is crown'd
With immortality, who fears to follow
Where airy voices lead. . . .
— JOHN KEATS
"Endymion"

Jenko's Prologue

I MAY BE BLIND as an oyster, but I can tell there's a full moon out tonight. My fever has broken and I feel awash in a cool glow.

I'm sitting now at my desk by the window, and I can hear all the familiar voices of the waterfront. It's that magical time of night here between two worlds; the bars have closed and the drunks have staggered off singing, yet the fishermen have not yet arrived with their clomping boots and jangling oarlocks.

Listen! Can you hear the boats straining their lines and rubbing against the pilings? How about the drowsy barking of the sea lions out on the breakwater? Or the muffled *dong-g-g!* of the bell buoy tolling in the tide?

I've grown old with these sounds. They've comforted me many a night while working late. I'm a sculptor by trade and I've lived and labored here on the wharf for much of my eighty-eight years. My name is Jenko.

For a while I was afraid I'd chiseled my last stone in this studio, that age and ailments had finally wrenched the mallet out of my hand. I fought them, mind you, right up until a few minutes ago. You should have seen me. Burning with fever and tangled up in my damp nightshirt, I was thrashing in bed like a fish in a sea bird's beak.

Don't worry, I'm fine now. In fact, I got up feeling spry as a porpoise pup. And after hearing the friendly creaks and splashings outside, I had the urge to throw my own voice into the night. That's why I'm writing. I want to tell you about this place and two boys who lived here years ago, back when my beard wasn't so white nor my head so bald and bumpy. Theirs is the story of the ghost of Fisherman's Wharf.

It doesn't bother me if you're skeptical about spooks. I didn't believe in them either. That's why I never really understood this story, even though I myself lived through it. But it all came clear to me tonight in the throes of my delirium.

So let me begin and I promise to finish before dawn drains this peaceful puddle of moonlight. . . .

CHAPTER ONE
The Secret Shed

IT ALL BEGAN on Columbus Day, 1955. It was the day of the unveiling, a beautiful day. A storm had just passed and the October air was so crisp and fresh it tickled your nostrils. The seagulls were out in full force, screeching like an off-key chorus. They circled high above the wharf, caught up in the intoxicating aroma of seafood, pizza, caramel corn and gun powder.

"Aye-aye-aye!" cried the birds as they eyed the curious spectacle below. Some of the braver gulls, angling for a closer look and perhaps a scrap to eat, spiralled down to the sagging, guano-streaked rooftops.

American flags flapped briskly outside the many restaurants, gift shops, and art galleries that bordered the old T-shaped pier. Sightseers were everywhere. Some leaned over the railings to feed the sea lions or photograph the boats rocking in the bay. Others strolled around window-shopping and eating cotton candy or shrimp cocktails. Pigeons cooed and clustered at the feet of anyone who paused to feed them.

Visiting sport fishermen also lumbered by, toting their poles and dragging gunny sacks bulging with fish. Most of the old Italian commercial fishermen were here too, but they had taken the day off and were dressed in their Sunday best.

Oddly, the only one at work was Babe, a rosy-cheeked

paisano known as the laziest fisherman in town. He was wearing black Frisco jeans and a plaid work shirt—the unofficial uniform of Monterey Bay fishermen. Always a late riser, Babe rarely caught enough fish to pay for his fuel. But that didn't stop him from trying, and he was now happily repainting his lampara boat, the *Pippina Louise,* which was up on chocks at Hooper's Dry Dock. Some of his fishermen friends stood around joking as they watched him work.

"Hey, Babe, you missed a spot," one of them teased.

"Yeah, you no careful justa 'cause your bosses on holiday," called another.

Babe gave his paint-filled brush a good shake in their direction and the men scattered. He never paid any attention to their talk, but he did look around now for his two young "bosses," Cosmo and Sammy Serafino. The brothers had helped him all week but hadn't yet shown up today. I wonder what they're up to, thought Babe.

That same thought also passed through the mind of Sergeant Abner, the portly, white haired policeman who was stationed in the little booth at the wharf's entrance. He could hear firecrackers exploding in the distance and he wondered if it wasn't Cosmo and Sammy. It worried him, for the old pier had been built by a steamship company around the turn of the century and its old, dry timbers were highly flammable. Sergeant Abner wanted to go after whoever was shooting off the firecrackers but he was too busy at the moment handing out maps to the tourists, turning away delivery trucks, and performing all the tasks of his pre-retirement post.

No one else seemed to share Abner's concern; they were too busy enjoying the festivities or catering to customers. Indeed, all of the wharf merchants were plying a fierce holiday trade, and none more so than Benny the organ grinder and Buffa, his capuchin monkey. Benny, who sported a huge handlebar mustache, was fresh from Sicily, but he could have passed for native-born today. Both he and Buffa were outfitted in the patriot costumes they had gotten for the Fourth of July. They wore tri-corn'd hats, long blue coats, ruffled shirts and knickers. As Benny cranked out the tune of "Yankee Doodle," Buffa danced from one group of open palms to another, collecting her due.

The crowd was amazed at the monkey's intelligence. "She sure knows her coins," commented one man. And it was true. When handed a copper penny, Buffa would bite it to make sure it was real and then stuff it in the green pouch hanging from her belt. When she got a nickel, she'd shake the hand it came from. And for a dime she'd tip her hat and bow.

Just then a little girl dropped a quarter into Buffa's hand. The monkey paused for a second and then sprang up and thanked her with a kiss on the lips that shocked the girl and sent squeals of laughter rippling through the crowd.

It was the same up and down the wharf—everyone performed for the tourists' dollars. At Prince's Sea Trips, for example, a young deckhand was valiantly trying to outbark the sea lions: "Get your tickets here for the bay cruise," he hollered, hands cupped around his mouth. "See the sights of beautiful Monterey Bay. See the sea lions, sea otters, China Point and Cannery Row. Get your tickets here!"

Across the way at the Wharf Theater, a crowd was filing in to catch a matinee of the new musical, *Anchors Aweigh.* And next door at Angelo's bar and restaurant, Angelo himself, in a white apron and bow tie, was passing out free wine and balloons to the people in his waiting line. Now Angelo was by nature a stingy sort, but he had learned that a calculated show of generosity was good for business.

Opposite Angelo's was Ratzo's Fish Market, where another group of tourists had gathered. Rows of fish were neatly laid out as usual on a table of shaved ice. But at the foot of the table was a shark's head with jaws open wide, revealing rows of razor-sharp teeth. Strung up directly above the shark was a purple octopus with long suction-cupped tentacles. Babe had caught them both just before the storm and sold them to Ratzo, who shrewdly kept them in the cooler until now to give his market an edge over the others. The plan seemed to be paying off, for the market was swamped with customers, and Ratzo, his wife and their crew were rushing around like crazy in their rubber boots and aprons.

Even old Gao, the Chinese fish peddler, was doing a brisk, although not quite legal, business. His game today was buying from the sport fishermen, who were not licensed to sell their catch. He greeted them all as they stepped off Prince's party boat, which had just docked at one of the cross piers. "Extra fish today?" asked Gao as he stroked his flowing white mustache and smiled slyly from beneath his big straw cowboy hat. Gao carried a bamboo shoulder pole, and dangling from each end were the baskets he used to peddle his fish door-to-door down the peninsula.

POW-POW-POW-POW-POW! A string of firecrackers suddenly exploded under old Gao's feet. He hopped and yelled and covered his face as a gang of young pranksters ran laughing down an alley and disappeared behind a boarded-up packing house.

Old Gao was still pulling on his ears and trying to get his hearing back when a quartet of black-suited musicians at the wharf's intersection struck up a tarantella. The band played on a make-shift stage behind a sheet-draped figure tied with rope. The swift and delirious music of their mandolin, accordion, drum and cornet filled the air and sent hundreds of townspeople rushing over to dance arm-in-arm. Locked in the tempo, the dancers skipped and spun in a glorious pinwheel of color. The tourists clapped and cheered them on.

Caught up in all the excitement, even the gulls cried out louder than ever.

Suddenly, from beneath the bouncing planks rose the blackened faces of Cosmo and Sammy, squinting from the bright sunlight. They pulled themselves up quick as eels, slithered under the railing, and began running—backwards— up the wharf.

Bellies astern, the boys raced through the crowd past Angelo's and the theater, past the gift shops and the art galleries. Cosmo, who had longer, stronger legs and a knack for dodging obstacles of all kinds, pulled ahead of his younger brother. Sammy tried to speed up but the adults blocked his way. Losing sight of Cosmo, he backpedalled even faster.

Sammy then spotted a clear passage in front of Ratzo's market and veered toward it. But Ratzo appeared all at once from behind the ice table wheeling a low crate of soaking squid. Too late to stop or swerve, Sammy's heels struck the box and he went sprawling headfirst into the inky, icy water. His splash drenched Ratzo and all of the bystanders, whose screams rang through the market. Sammy was floundering amid the squids' eyeballs and tentacles when Ratzo plucked him up by the hair.

"What the devil you doing?" he shouted, and rocked the boy with a rubber-booted kick to the pants.

"Leave him be," yelled Cosmo, breaking through the crowd.

"Humph! I'll fix both you wharf rats," growled the burly market boss. And he called back to his workers, "Grab that one."

Cosmo quickly scooped a handful of ice off the table and as

one of Ratzo's teenaged helpers came forward, Cosmo blasted him in the face with it. Another worker, a tall guy with a shaved head, came up behind Cosmo and grabbed him by the neck. Cosmo tried to wriggle free, but the man held tight.

"Leggo," said Cosmo in a choked voice. He beat on the man's arms but it had no effect. Then Cosmo's fist brushed the octopus and he knew in an instant what to do. Cosmo grabbed onto a tentacle and pulled the octopus onto the man's head. The bald guy cried out and reached up to pull the thing off, letting Cosmo free. Sammy slipped out of Ratzo's grasp at that same moment and the two boys ran off—frontwards—with the crew sloshing after them in their clumsy boots, cursing all the while.

Cosmo and Sammy ducked under the chain in front of Hooper's, flew past Babe, and tore down the stairs to the lower dock. The tide was high and it swashed all around the narrow strip of planks. Skiffs dangled from ropes and pulleys between the outer pilings. Moss-fringed ladders dipped below the waterline.

The boys clattered across the damp boards, and the beat and squeak of their sneakers echoed off the low ceiling of the upper dock. The planks dropped off in an apparent dead-end, but Cosmo and Sammy kept going, running up and down the lower halves of the x-shaped crossbeams that connected the pilings. Without once bothering to look back, they plunged deeper and deeper into the shadowy maze of timbers that supported the old pier.

Although it was quite forbidding to most people, Cosmo and Sammy felt at home under the wharf. It was their turf, their kingdom, and few dared trespass. Only an occasional crew of plumbers, who had originally laid the pipes and catwalks that now served as their highway, ever ventured into the interior. Generally, it was much too cramped and dirty down there for adults, especially to give chase.

Town kids avoided the area, too. Their parents had frightened them with lies that rats lurked behind every beam, and that in days past children had fallen off the slippery planks and drowned in the swirling green seawater, never to be seen again.

Only Cosmo and Sammy fearlessly explored these nether regions. They *liked* to think of themselves as wharf rats, and were no more afraid of slipping off a plank than Buffa the monkey would fear falling out of a tree. Since coming to Monterey three years earlier, the boys had roamed from one end of the wharf's underbelly to the other, without incident. Their Aunt Nastina had ordered the area off limits, of course, but she was usually much too busy to enforce this rule.

The brothers traveled quickly along the crossbeams and brace-boards. The farther they got from the edge, the thicker the air grew with the sweet, briny stink of starfish and wet wood. Less and less light fell on their path; only a few determined rays now slipped between the barnacle-encrusted pilings. The footsteps and voices of the tourists could be heard through the planks, but they were muffled by the constant splashing of drains emptying into the bay. Cosmo and Sammy knew well how to avoid the slimy boards placed under these drains.

Finally, they crossed one last set of beams, swung hand-over-hand on a thick iron pipe, and lowered themselves onto a tiny platform. Here, hidden in the bowels of the wharf, was their secret shed.

"I guess we lost 'em," said Cosmo, pulling a rusty sixteen-penny nail from the latch. The door squeaked open and the boys waded into the darkness.

Sammy felt for the coffee can on the shelf where they kept the matches and spare candles. He found a pack and lit the red drip candle that was stuck in a wine bottle on the table. The light cast a dim glow over the shed, which was furnished with just the table and two stools—actually an old telephone-wire spool and two wooden clam boxes. But scattered about were cork bobbers, coils of rope, a broken propeller, and lots of other junk. It was so cluttered, in fact, that there was hardly any room for the boys, especially Cosmo, whose head came right up to the ceiling.

He and Sammy couldn't have made the shed any larger, however, because they had found the platform and merely walled it in with wood from old fish crates and the nails they had picked up when the theater was being built. Cosmo had even salvaged a whole piece of glass, which he installed as a window. But it was now so caked with salt and grime that they couldn't see through it.

Beside the window was tacked a torn snapshot of a handsome couple standing in front of a sailboat. They were Cosmo and Sammy's parents, who had drowned when their boat sank in a squall off Gloucester. Sammy had retrieved the photo out of the garbage after Aunt Nastina, who came east to fetch the boys, had gone through the family belongings. Sammy remembered her saying she didn't ever want to be reminded of the boat or its foolhardy skipper.

Sammy looked over at his brother, who had sprawled out on the pile of fishnet in the corner. Unlike Sammy, who was ten, Cosmo was big for his age, which was twelve. He had grown a lot that year and his clothes showed it. His pants stopped short of his ankles and his yellow T-shirt stretched tight over his shoulders.

In other ways, the boys resembled each other. Both had curly brown hair, light olive skin, and high, round cheeks. But where those features looked angelic on Sammy, they suggested a certain mischievousness in Cosmo. He was now sitting up with his hands behind his head and smirking contentedly. Sammy couldn't stand that look.

"What's so funny?" he asked.

"Nothing," said Cosmo, obviously proud of his exploits.

"It's your fault, you know."

"What?"

"What do you mean 'what'? I told you it was too crowded to race like that."

"Hey, I made it okay. Just be glad I came back when I did."

"Glad! We're in worse trouble now. Next time Ratzo sees us, we're all through. I don't know how we can even risk going to Jenko's unveiling."

"Ah, relax."

"You can relax, you're not all soaking wet."

Cosmo grinned at his brother, who stood pathetically in an ever-widening puddle of his own making. Candlelight glistened off Sammy's matted curls and sopping clothes. His bottom lip puffed out and his large, dark eyes swelled with tears. He started to say something, but then a worried look crossed his dripping brow. Sammy thrust his hand down his shirt and pulled out a wet, rubbery squid. Cosmo started laughing and Sammy hurled it at him. Cosmo quickly slouched out of the way and the squid smacked against the wall behind him and stuck.

"Hey, watch out. You're making a mess," shouted Cosmo. "Don't be such a baby."

"Don't you be such a jerk," shouted Sammy.

The boys glared at each other, on the verge of one of their frequent fights. Then Sammy leaped onto Cosmo and got him in a headlock. "You're getting me all wet," yelled

Cosmo as he tried to twist out of it. They both tumbled off the net and onto the floor, with Sammy still on top. He grabbed hold of Cosmo's fingers and was bending them back when his brother howled and pushed him off with both feet.

"All right, all right," said Cosmo. "It wasn't the greatest idea. What do you want me to do about it now?"

"Nothing," said Sammy, getting up and plunking himself down on a stool.

"Come on. Don't worry about Ratzo. He'll cool off. He always does."

"Huh, not today he won't."

Cosmo scooted back onto the net and shook out his sore fingers. "Tell you what; I got another idea. Just to be safe we'll go to the unveiling in disguise. Okay?"

Sammy looked up, interested. "What kind of disguise?"

"Just trust me."

"Yeah, that's what you always say," moaned Sammy.

"What are you talking about?" snapped Cosmo.

"Remember, you said it the time we sold Angelo all those clams we dug up."

"So?"

"So everybody he served 'em to got sick."

"He shoulda known they were outa season," reasoned Cosmo.

"And you said it that day you made me get in one of Ratzo's fish crates to see if we could use it for a boat," Sammy continued.

"I pulled you out after it sank, didn't I?" countered Cosmo.

"Pull-shmull," replied Sammy. "You even said it just before we raced, and look what happened?"

"What? Nothing! An afternoon bath."

Sammy looked down at his dripping clothes. He shook his

head in resignation. "All right," he said. "But these disguises better be good."

"Relax, I told you. I'll come up with just the thing. But first you got to do something for me."

"What?" asked Sammy.

"Go home and change," said Cosmo, holding his nose.

CHAPTER TWO
The Skiff's Rescue

AFTER CLOSING up the shed, the boys swung from pipe to piling until they emerged from under the landing behind Aunt Nastina's Lighthouse Gift Shop, over which they lived.

Cosmo sat down against the back fence to wait while Sammy stripped on the stairs and wheeled his clothes out to dry on the squeaky clothesline. Sammy peeked inside the door to make sure his aunt wasn't home, and then bounded naked up the spiral staircase to his and Cosmo's bedroom in the tower.

The room was hot and stuffy and Sammy opened one of its many curved windows. Although the little tower had never served as an actual lighthouse, it did overlook the entire bay. The coastline stretched for miles in the gentle arc of an abalone shell, with the sweeping white beaches to the north gradually giving way to the rocky arm of China Point.

There in the middle, where granite boulders littered the sandy shore, the wharf jutted out proudly. It was actually an extension of Monterey's main street. The town itself was a mere cluster of buildings set apart by weed-cracked avenues and overshadowed by the bell tower of the Mission San Carlos. Beyond were pine-covered hills sprinkled with white-washed houses.

Between downtown and the wharf was the old Custom

House, where in days past traders registered their goods and exchanged news of previous ports o' call. The two-story adobe had since been converted into a museum, with a pair of sun-bleached whale ribs and a salvaged bronze anchor mounted beneath its portico. But its grounds remained a gathering place for oldtimers to swap tales while mending nets or playing bocce ball.

A set of railroad tracks stitched around the edge of the peninsula and, to the south, cut through the abandoned buildings of Cannery Row. Once the economic heart of Monterey, these boarded-up fish factories now stood idle, their cold, smokeless stacks and corregated warehouses rusting silently over the tidepools.

Unseen about a mile offshore was the notorious Monterey Trench. Oceanographers had never successfully sounded its depths, but they estimated that the Grand Canyon was a mere gully in comparison. Local folks tended to think of the trench as bottomless. They told stories about how it swallowed up skiffs and freighters alike, without so much as a bubbly belch.

Yet it was the deep waters and constant upwelling that made Monterey Bay such a rich fishing ground. Generations of Chinese, Italian, Portuguese, Slovak and other immigrants settled here and reaped its silver harvest.

Unfortunately for them all, the boom days of fishing ended in 1950 when the sardine industry went belly up. Oh, some fishermen still managed to make a living going for salmon, squid and albacore, but it wasn't like before when they'd all catch tons of sardines every night and return home with their wallets fat. The canneries on the Row would smoke around the clock and the pungent smell of fish wafted through the whole town. But nobody complained, for it was called "the stink of prosperity."

Then one night it happened—none of the fishermen could locate a school of the shiny pilchards. Week after week they tried, dropping their nets and winching them up empty. To this day no one knows why or where the sardines went. Babe claims they swam away when the currents changed. Ratzo says they were plain fished out. But whatever the reason, the canneries closed down one by one and most of the fishermen drifted into other work.

That's when the wharf began to change, too. Angelo and his brothers, for example, sold their boat and bought an old warehouse which they converted into the first seafood restaurant on the wharf. For this they would go down in local history as pioneers of the first order.

Soon after, fish-packing sheds gave way to gift shops, and net-tanning tanks were replaced with art galleries. Sightseers started streaming in and tourism became the industry of the future.

The old days now blended with the new, and never more so than on Columbus Day. It was a time when Monterey's Italian community turned out to celebrate its seafaring heritage. Every year more and more tourists flocked to take part in the festivities. And the ironic result was that the holiday, while honoring the past, speeded the old fishing pier's rebirth into a swaying carnival-over-the-sea.

Sammy had given himself a spitbath, put on another set of baggy hand-me-downs, and was brushing the knots out of his hair when—KABOOM!—an explosion made him fling the brush across the room.

He ran to the window and spotted a group of boys laughing and shoving each other on the beach. Sammy didn't know it, but it was the same gang that had tossed the firecrackers at old Gao. Down below, Cosmo also was watching them from over the fence.

A big redheaded, freckle-faced kid ordered the other five boys quiet and squatted to unwrap some newspaper which contained three squids. Holding one out, the redhead called to the gulls that had flown up to the rooftops after the explosion.

"Come he-e-e-re, you old licebags," he beckoned in a phony sing-songy voice. "I've got a surpri-i-yise."

The redhead threw the squid in the air and as soon as it hit the water three gulls swooped down on it. The biggest bird pecked it up and flew back to the roof, where all the others snapped and yapped for a piece.

A sinister chuckle rumbled out of the boy's fat, freckled belly. "There's more where that came from, ya greedy scavengers. Gimme the cherry bomb," he said, turning to a skinny kid who was sitting on an old skiff that had washed ashore in the recent storm. The boy reached into a paper bag and pulled out a thick, red firecracker. The redhead grabbed it and stuffed it inside the squid, leaving only the long fuse exposed.

"Let's have some fire," he said.

With a trembling hand, the skinny kid struck a wooden match and lit the fuse. The redhead quickly threw the sizzling squid-stick of dynamite high over the water. The gang cowered for cover behind the skiff and watched as the seagulls raced down as before.

This time an all-white gull beat the flock and in one graceful motion swooped down, gulped up the squid, and curved upward. Just as it pumped its wings to gain greater height, the cherry bomb exploded and the bird's head and chest burst into a million bloody flecks. Feathers flew everywhere, and the remaining carcass smacked hard against the surface of the sea.

"Ha, ha, did you see that? BABOOM! Just like I told you guys," cheered the redhead. "Do you think they'll fall for it again?"

Sammy stood horrified at the window, but Cosmo shook off his shock and climbed on top of the fence. Standing straight up, thirty feet above the rocky tide pools, he called down to the gang, "Get your scummy selves outa here!"

Cosmo's deep voice carried in the wind and the gang boys looked up fearfully. Seeing that the intruder was younger and smaller than he was, the redhead let out a big belly laugh. "Take a dive," he said.

"I'm telling you to scat before I stuff the next one down *your* throat," hollered Cosmo.

The redhead laughed again and looked at his pals for support. One by one they forced out pathetic little titters. Satisfied with this show of solidarity, the redhead said, "Come and try it."

In the next instant Cosmo ran the length of the wobbly fence, leaped to the metal clothesline post and slid down it. Then he dropped to a plank beneath the wharf, traversed the bouncing board, hopped to a seaweed draped cross-beam, jumped to a boulder, and landed in the sand—face-to-face with the gang leader.

"Ah, that was nothing," scowled the boy, obviously surprised by Cosmo's skill and daring. The redhead lunged at him with a wild punch to the face. Cosmo side stepped his attacker and socked him hard behind the ear, knocking him to the sand.

Cosmo turned to the skinny kid holding the bag of firecrackers and held out his hand for them. The boy hesitated and Cosmo clenched his fist threateningly. Then he snatched the bag with his other hand. None of the other kids dared move from behind the wrecked skiff.

Meantime, the redhead had climbed to one knee and was spitting sand. When he saw Cosmo with his bag of firecrackers, he yelled, "Get him, guys! I paid a lot for that stuff."

The boys suddenly jumped to their feet and surrounded Cosmo.

"We'll teach you to mind your own business," swore the redhead as he joined his friends.

"Shut up and start swinging," spat Cosmo, trying to sound like a battle-starved pirate. In truth, he was mad at himself for getting into such a predicament. He wondered how he had ever expected to take on a whole gang by himself.

Cosmo knew he needed an equalizer and looked around desperately for one. He saw a splintered oar over in the tide pools, but it was too far away. His only hope was to reach a nearby clump of seaweed. He kicked sand at the boys and made a break for it. He got there just ahead of them and grabbed a long piece of bull kelp. Cracking it like a whip, he yelled, "Come any closer and I'll scale you from head to toe."

The gang stopped cold and looked to their leader for orders. "He's bluffing," said the redhead, and he pushed his skinny friend forward. Cosmo lashed him across the legs. The stinging snap of seaweed sounded like a bolt of lightning, and the boy began yelping with pain.

"You show 'em, Coz," yelled Sammy from the window.

Cosmo grinned. "Who's next?" he challenged, and unwisely cracked the kelp again as a warning. This time it snapped, and he was left holding a harmless little stump. "Uh-oh," he said.

"Now we got you," gloated the redhead.

The gang fanned out and stalked Cosmo to the water's edge. He dropped the piece of kelp but tightened his grip on the bag of firecrackers. He soon felt the sea's froth lapping at his heels. But as the six youths closed in, he noticed a man zig-zagging down the steep embankment to the beach. Cosmo's mind, racing with fear, latched onto an idea.

"We'll destroy you," Cosmo growled. Then he yelled to the man who was now tramping across the sand. "Don't even hurry, Pop!" The gang boys shot frightened glances at the nearing adult, at Cosmo, and then at each other.

"We'll take care of you later," declared the redhead. "Let's go, guys." And the gang took off on the run up the beach.

"Phew!" Cosmo sighed loudly and took a deep breath which puffed him up with a sense of conquest. He stuffed the bag in his back pocket and was smiling stupidly when his "Pop" approached the skiff.

The man was obviously a fisherman. His broad, swaying shoulders were thrust forward as if he was walking against a gale. He wore dark, heavy clothes and a gray cap that cast a shadow over his beard-stubbled face. His breath smelled like liquor.

The fisherman paid no mind to Cosmo but went about inspecting the skiff. He kicked its sides, rapped its bottom, and sucked its joints for moisture. Then he spat and cursed in Italian.

"*Figlia du buta . . .* " he swore, stopping short when he noticed Cosmo watching him. "*E' finito.* " he said, shaking his head.

"Can't you fix her?" asked Cosmo.

The fisherman shrugged. "Bah! What for? De old t'ing stinka like rot. Is not wortha da trouble. You wanna? I kiss g'bye. Is all yours." He turned and trudged off the same way he had come.

"Really?" cried Cosmo. But the fisherman kept walking. "Thanks," Cosmo yelled after him. "Thanks a lot!" And he climbed into the boat and whooped for joy. "C'mon," he waved to Sammy. "We got ourselves a skiff."

Sammy waved back and in his excitement climbed right out the window. He dropped to the roof, slid down a drain pipe, and then ran off the wharf to meet Cosmo.

The brothers worked fast. Butts in the air, they shoveled sand through their legs with both hands, tirelessly trying to rescue the boat from its early grave. They were afraid the gang would return at any moment or that the fisherman would change his mind and take back their prized skiff.

"I can't believe he just gave her away," said Cosmo between scoops. "Sure she needs work, but we can do it. We'll slap a plywood patch here and there and then caulk her up nice and tight. After a paint job, she'll be like new."

"Keep digging," said Sammy. "Over here more."

"Once she's fixed," Cosmo went on, "we'll be able to go anywhere, do anything. We could just guide her through the pilings instead of always climbing to the shed and worrying about keeping the way secret. And we could go fishing out past the breakwater, lay nets even. There's just no end to what we can do now that we got a skiff."

With the sideboards fully exposed, the two boys rocked the little eight-foot boat back and forth until its flat bottom broke free of the sand's damp grip.

"Now go fetch that piece of oar in the rocks over there," directed Cosmo.

Sammy hurried over to the tide pools, where he noticed something that looked like a charred mop floating in the shallows. He suddenly felt queasy, realizing that the soggy black clump was all that remained of the white gull. Sammy's stomach roiled, but he couldn't look away. He watched as though in a trance as the dead bird drifted out with the tide.

Finally, he snapped his eyes free, gathered up the splintered oar, and ran back to the skiff.

After wedging the oar midway under the skiff, Cosmo took hold of the bow and Sammy stationed himself at the stern. At the count of three they gave it a heave-ho—pushing, pulling, and sputtering out groans. The little boat jerked forward and rolled over the rod as if on coasters.

Cosmo winked confidently at his brother and brought the oar up front. Then he and Sammy put their backs into it again—and again—and again. They blistered their palms and flooded their shoes with sand, but their grit and teamwork propelled the skiff steadily across the beach. They stopped to rest only when they reached the embankment.

"What'll we name her?" asked Sammy.

"Hmm . . . I don't know," said Cosmo. "How about *Whisky Breath,* after that fisherman?"

"Don't be a dumbbell."

"Well, then how about the *Santa Maria,* after Columbus' pilot ship? This is the day he discovered America, you know."

"You don't say?" mocked Sammy. "I thought it was the day he fell outa the crow's nest."

"You got a better idea, wise guy?"

"Yeah, why don't we name her after the seagull those guys killed. You know, just to pay respects."

Cosmo thought about it seriously. "Maybe," he said. "Or we could name her after Mom. That's what Babe did."

"We'll think of something," said Sammy.

Cosmo now suggested a new way to proceed. He and Sammy rolled the skiff over and over, and it advanced up the slope with each turn. Near the top, however, Sammy lost his grip and the boat lurched dangerously.

"Watch out!" he yelled to Cosmo, who was standing on the downside. It was too late. The overturned skiff skidded into Cosmo and pitched him up in the air. He landed with a thud on top of the speeding skiff-sled and clung to its keel.

Sammy watched in horror as the thundering, rumbling craft careened down the hill on its gunnels, threatening to flip on any bump and crush his brother. Cosmo's bone-rattling ride ended at the foot of the hill with a terrific jolt that hurled him headlong into the sand.

"I thought you had her!" he fumed moments later, staggering to his feet.

"I did until *you* let go," Sammy shouted back.

The boys eventually shrugged off their misfortune and began rolling the boat uphill once again. They worked more carefully this time and before long the creaking skiff flopped safely on level ground. Their triumphant cheers resounded along the shore.

It was smooth sailing from there on. With Sammy rotating the oar and Cosmo pushing from astern, the skiff rode the rod easily onto the wharf and through a parting sea of gawking tourists.

"Think we should go in and tell Aunt Nastina we're gonna be working out back?" asked Sammy as they approached the gift shop.

"I guess so," said Cosmo. "She'll have a fit if she just stumbles onto us."

They leaned the little row boat against the wall and marched inside single file, arms pressed against their sides. This was the only position in which Aunt Nastina let her nephews enter the shop. She was firm about it and would have demanded the same from her customers except she knew she'd lose business. As a compromise, she tacked PLEASE DO NOT HANDLE and YOU BREAK IT, YOU BUY IT signs on almost every shelf.

Nevertheless, Sammy liked going into his aunt's shop, for it was filled with shiny brass storm lanterns, old fashioned spittoons, and all kinds of exotic stuff. Hanging over the bustling showroom was an enormous swan-neck chandelier with flame-shaped light bulbs and hundreds of dangling prisms which cast little dancing rainbows everywhere.

Sparkling in the display cases were pearl necklaces, rhinestone tiaras, gold lockets, and other jewelry. Ornately-framed mirrors lined the walls and doubled everything. Instead of two suits of armor, there were four. Instead of four grandfather clocks, there were eight. And instead of a dozen shoppers, there were oodles of them.

But best of all, in Sammy's opinion, was the section in the far corner brimming with fine, polished sea shells. There were turbos, conchs, chambered nautiluses, and even dried seahorses and spiney blowfish swaying on strings.

Ch-ch-Ding! The giant gold and black antique cash register on the front counter suddenly rang out above the customers' chatter. Gripping the crank was Aunt Nastina's hand which appeared garishly swollen due to the huge rings on every finger. She tapped out the price of an item and then spun the handle again with a sharp motion acquired through years of successful shopkeeping. Ch-ch-Ding!

Working the register, Aunt Nastina looked as eccentric as the merchandise she sold. A blue, high-necked gown swathed her boney frame. Bifocals balanced on the tip of her pointy nose. And a mound of bluish-white hair crowned the top of her head.

Aunt Nastina (her real name was Agnestina, but the boys mispronounced it from the very beginning) always wore tons of makeup, which Sammy thought was just right for once. As if in honor of Columbus' discovery of America, Nastina's thin lips were painted a bright red, her face powdered a chalky white, and her eyelids inked a deep blue.

"So there you are!" she screeched after finishing with her customer. "What's this I hear about disrupting Ratzo's market?"

Aunt Nastina had a crackling voice that sounded like the static on the fishermen's shortwave radios. What's more, she had the habit of buzzing on just as endlessly.

"It's the busiest day of the year and no one on the wharf has time for your nonsense," she continued, "least of all me. Lord knows I've tried. And my sister—rest her soul—must know. But you boys never learn . . ."

"But Aunty, we were just racing," cut in Sammy, "and I happened to fall in Ratzo's squid. It was an accident. Honest."

"Oh, and what about hitting that poor boy with the ice?" she asked Cosmo. "Was that an accident too?"

Cosmo gulped and stared up at the chandelier.

"Look at me when I talk to you," she said. "And what's the idea of running away under the wharf? Look at your clothes, they're filthy. How many times have I told you not to go down there?"

Cosmo spoke up: "We're sorry, Aunty, but we had to. They were after us."

"I don't have time for this," she cried, her hands raised pleadingly toward the heavens. "Go on now. What did you come in here for, anyway?"

"We wanted to ask permission for something," said Sammy. Cosmo nudged him and whispered, "Not now!"

"What?" snapped Aunt Nastina.

"Well, you see, we found a skiff," said Sammy, "and we want to fix her up out back."

"You'll do no such thing," said Aunt Nastina. "I need that area clear for deliveries."

"But no one ever . . . " began Sammy.

"Don't sass me back," said Nastina. "I said no and I mean it. Besides, for all I know you probably stole the thing."

"No we didn't," said Cosmo indignantly. "She was washed up on the beach and the owner came by and said we could have her."

"Well, I say you can't. And I don't want to hear any more about it."

"Aw, c'mon," begged Sammy. "Town kids all have bicycles. Ranch kids get horses. Why can't we have a row boat?"

"Yeah, Aunty," added Cosmo. "We could catch all our own fish, and even sell some to the markets. Think of it as a business venture."

"More like a drowning venture, you mean. Do you want to end up like your parents?"

The boys stood in silence and Aunt Nastina noticed some of her customers staring. "Now scram," she said. "You're getting sand all over the floor."

"Okay," said Cosmo, "but let us just fix her up and then we'll sell her. It would be a waste not to do that much."

"All right, all right," said Aunt Nastina. "But you'll have to find some place else to make your mess. And you're never to take it out on the water. Is that clear?"

"Sure, sure. Thanks a lot," said Cosmo as he hustled Sammy out the door.

"And don't go under the wharf!" yelled Aunt Nastina.

Once outside, Sammy shoved his brother away. "Let go," he said. "What's the big idea?"

"We had to get out of there before she changed her mind."

"Who cares if she does? Why should we fix a boat just to watch someone else get all the fun?"

"Don't worry about that. We'll work now and change her mind later."

"Where we gonna work?"

"Let's see if we can sneak it past Ratzo's and over to the dock behind Jenko's place. I've been doing him a favor for the last couple of months, so he should be glad to help us out."

CHAPTER THREE
The Unveiling

JENKO...? HEY, JENKO...? Are you up there?" called Cosmo as Sammy knocked on the open door.

There was no answer, only the faint sound of voices drifting through the dark stairwell. Suddenly, a hearty laugh surged downward.

"That's him all right," said Cosmo. "Let's go." And the brothers scrambled noisily up the narrow, wooden stairs.

Pausing at the top, they scanned the dimly-lit expanse of Jenko's neat but cluttered studio. The old sculptor was nowhere in sight. Only a few pigeons stirred from their roosts high in the rafters. Cosmo and Sammy again heard the swish-swash of distant voices, and followed them through the cool shadows of the workshop.

They passed thick tables mounted with vises, high shelves sagging with jars and cans, and a pegged tool rack stocked with files, rasps, mallets and chisels. Then they came to the area where Jenko stored his new materials and unfinished works. There were barrels of clay and a large trunk of Canadian yellow pine. Also awaiting the sculptor's magic touch was a half-carved figurehead for a ship, a saddled swordfish for a merry-go-round, and a bust-shaped block of marble.

Hanging on a nail on the back wall by the sink was Jenko's stained canvas apron. Next to it was a red curtain tacked over the doorway to his living quarters. Jenko's booming laugh sounded through it.

"Hey, Jenko, it's us," cried Cosmo as he pulled the curtain aside.

Standing in the room, grinning as usual, was the brawny, gray-bearded sculptor. He looked odd, though. Instead of his usual work clothes, he had on a black tweed coat and he was tying on a red tie.

Stranger still were the two astonishing women in the room. Sitting on the bed was a crowned queen dressed in purple velvet, and leaning against the desk by the window was a barefoot Indian maiden in a cotton clout laced with feathers and fish bones. A pendant of pure gold hung from her nose.

"Ho-ho, my friends! You're just in time to come with us," said Jenko. "Allow me to introduce Her Highness Queen Isabella of Spain, and Her Fineness, Miss Guanahani of the Arawaks."

The women nodded nobly and then giggled.

"Nice to meet ya," replied Cosmo with a low, sweeping bow. Sammy stood dumbstruck until Cosmo elbowed him.

"Yeah, nice to meet ya," repeated Sammy. Then he clapped his hands and shouted, "I know who you are! You were in the last play at the theater. Remember, Cosmo, the time the manager let me and you buy one ticket and share a seat?"

"But of course you know us," teased the queen. "I'm the one who sponsored Senor Cristobal Colon's fruitless search for the Indies."

"And it was I and my people who greeted him when he ran into our island by mistake," said the Indian.

"Yep, there's always the danger of finding new worlds when you sail unknown seas," said Jenko, his sightless gray eyes twinkling. "But I'm sure you ladies have forgiven Columbus his failures, since you've both agreed to take part in today's little pageant and act as my royal escorts. Shall we go? It seems we've been waiting centuries for this day. Heh, heh, isn't that right, Cosmo? Have you been able to keep our little secret?"

Cosmo nodded.

"Good," said Jenko.

"What is this great secret?" asked Miss Guanahani.

"The sooner we go, the sooner you'll know," answered Jenko.

"Wait a minute," said Sammy. "Coz and me want to know if we can use your dock to work on the skiff we found today. She's there now and it doesn't take up much room. We won't make a mess either. Can we?"

"So that's what brings you around; you've got the boat you've been hoping for. You know, I was a master shipwright in my younger days, before I lost my eyes. I'd love to be of help, but I can only do so on one condition."

"Anything," cried Sammy.

"You both must take me along on your maiden voyage."

"Heck yes!" exclaimed Sammy.

"Of course," said Cosmo, both forgetting their promise to Aunt Nastina.

Jenko laughed loud and long. Then the queen checked her wristwatch. "Let's go," she cried. "We're due on stage now."

On their way out, Cosmo stopped suddenly. "I almost forgot," he said. "Sammy and I need costumes, too."

"Oh, why of course you do," said Jenko. "Let's see what I can rustle up real quick."

Down on the wharf, Jenko's sheet-draped statue stood center-stage like a little ghost while hundreds of holiday rollickers swarmed around. The band had stopped playing and people

in the crowd were stretching their necks and balancing on
tiptoes to better view the covered object.

"That Jenko smells of genius a mile off," Babe told Ratzo.
"I can't wait to see what he's come up with."

"It'd better be good," replied Ratzo. "Some of us around
here weren't so sure his type of genius could be trusted with
the job."

Just then the cornet player in the band stood up and
sounded a regal greeting as a brigade of Knights of Columbus
from the mission marched two abreast down the wharf. The
points of their silver swords rose high and the golden plumes
on their hats trailed in the breeze.

Behind them scurried three small girls wearing cardboard
replicas of Columbus' ships: the *Nina, Pinta,* and *Santa Maria*
bobbed from their shoulders on tiny suspenders.

Then came a big-nosed man playing Christopher Columbus
himself. The navigator strode proudly through the crowd in
his velvet cloak and satin doublet. His square jaw jutted out
of the white ruffled collar and a floppy purple beret drooped
stylishly over his right eye.

Following Columbus in a donkey cart was the portly mayor
of Monterey, who waved his silk hat at all the people and
smiled so broadly that his jowls twitched.

When they had all mounted the stage, Columbus raised his
hand for silence. Everyone obeyed; even the seals and gulls
seemed to cease their droning. As in a pantomine, the silence
magnified Columbus' every gesture. Signalling the band with
a nod, he hurled his hand downward with great flourish and
burst out in song.

Columbus' rich tenor voice split the sky. He sang a popular
Italian aria about a lovestruck seafarer, and his performance
overwhelmed the people of Monterey. The music filled their
ears, flooded their hearts, and made them drunk with nostalgia.

Everyone except old Gao, that is, who stood, arms crossed, in the back muttering something about a "big phony." Yet after the final cadence, shouts of "Bravo! Bravo! Bravissimo!" rose from the crowd. Columbus bowed with great flourish.

Amid the ovation, another odd procession cut through the crowd. It was Jenko and his escorts, Miss Guanahani and Queen Isabella. Leading them was a huge swordfish in a red cloak.

"Make way," ordered the fish. "Make way for Jenko the sculptor!"

Actually, it was Cosmo wearing the *papier-mâche* head that Jenko had made before carving the fish for the merry-go-round. The tail, of course, was Sammy wrapped in Jenko's curtain.

They reached the stage, breathless. The swordfish waited on the steps near the donkey while Jenko and the women went up and shook hands with Columbus and the mayor. Then the mayor pulled out a fistful of papers from his breast pocket.

"Thank you, thank you," he said, as if the cheering had been for him. And he began to read:

"The concourse assembled here today is actuated by a spirit of gratitude toward the memory of one of Italy's noblest sons. Prolific as she has been in poets, heroes, philosophers and sages, no name in her annals, nor in those of other lands, has attained a higher place, as a benefactor of mankind, throughout the civilized world, than that of Christopher Columbus. . . . "

"How long do we have to listen to this?" whispered Sammy.

"Relax," said Cosmo. "He'll be finished soon."

As if on cue, a gust of wind swept the intersection of the wharf and stripped the mayor's speech out of his grasp. The pages flew high over his head and he nearly tumbled off the stage flailing after them. He came up empty-handed, however, and flushed red as if the gust had left him naked before his constituents.

"Er . . . a . . . let's get on with this thing," said the mayor. "As you all know, the town has asked Mr. Jenko here to fashion for us a statue of Christopher Columbus as a tribute to his indomitable spirit, which is so evidently shared by the citizens of Monterey."

The mayor now leaned toward the actresses and whispered, "Would he like to speak?"

"Why don't you ask him?" said the queen.

"He may not see too well," added the Indian, "but he hears fine."

The mayor turned to Jenko and said, "Would you like to say a few words, sir?"

"Yes, just a few," said Jenko, stepping to the front of the stage. "I would like to thank you all for favoring me with the commission. It was a challenge I took very seriously. I began by reading up on my subject—with the help of my friends, Queen Isabella of Spain and Miss Guanahani of the Arawaks."

The audience chuckled as the women took their bows.

"I came to appreciate Columbus' skill and courage as a navigator," said Jenko, "which did indeed change the course of history. But I also learned about the man's darker side, and the murder and enslavement of thousands of the Arawak people he called Indians."

A nervous murmur ran through the crowd.

"So my challenge was to create something that would be true to Columbus' remarkable vision and energy, but not celebrate his misdeeds. I hope I succeeded. The work must speak for itself now."

"Yes, hmmm," piped in the mayor. "Will Queen Isabella and Miss Guana . . . Guana . . . goulash please do the honors?"

"Gladly," said the Indian. "And the name is Guana*hani!*"

"Yes, of course, dear. So sorry."

While the two women untied the rope that held the sheet in place, Sammy, peeking under the cloak, noticed a new disturbance in the crowd. It was Aunt Nastina pushing her way to the front. And the last person she bumped was the red-headed kid that Cosmo had scuffled with on the beach.

Sammy shook his brother's knee and pointed toward the gull killer. Looking through the swordfish's mouth, Cosmo spotted him. Cosmo felt for the bag of firecrackers still tucked in his back pocket. Then he saw that the redhead was flanked by twice as many gang members as before.

"Uh-oh," said Cosmo. "Head for the shed as soon as the sheet flies."

With a rapid roll of the drum, Queen Isabella and Miss Guanahani took hold of the sheet's edge. They raised it high over their heads, paused for the dramatic effect actresses love, and then yanked it off. Beneath the billowing sheet emerged a life-sized statue of . . . COSMO!

Cries of astonishment rang out. Even Sammy gasped at the sight of the statue. Jenko shifted uneasily as all eyes absorbed his creation for the first time.

Clad only in cutoffs, the varnished wooden figure stood poised on the end of a pier. One arm cradled a globe and the other pointed toward the horizon. Its husky build, high cheeks, and curly hair were unmistakably Cosmo's.

Sammy looked up through the mask at his brother's face. The only difference between it and the statue was that Cosmo's eyes looked back while the statue's stared into space.

"So that's your secret!" said Sammy.

Cosmo nodded, and then turned his attention back toward the gang of town kids.

"Th-th-there must be some mistake," stammered the mayor.

"We commissioned you to sculpt a monument to Columbus, not of some child playing with a ball."

"No, no," said Jenko. "That's a globe. And it is Columbus—as a boy when he roamed the quays of Genoa. It was there that he pestered the seamen with his endless questions and dared to dream the dreams that would take him to the New World."

"What possessed you, man? That's not what we paid you for," rebuked the mayor.

"But that's the essence of Columbus at his best," argued Jenko, "the keen, questing, uncorrupted spirit of youth."

"It's nothing but a tribute to the biggest troublemaker on the wharf," shouted Ratzo.

"I'm so embarrassed," wailed Aunt Nastina. "How could you do such a thing?"

"It's an insult!" said Columbus.

"We've been had!" charged one of the knights.

"Give it the deep-six," hollered the redhead. "Heave it off the wharf."

"This won't do, this won't do at all," cried the mayor. "I'll have to call a meeting. We must assemble the council."

"Well, I think it's terrific," yelled Cosmo, throwing off the swordfish head and standing defiantly on the top step. A hush swept over the ceremony. It was broken only by the sound of Jenko chuckling.

"Let's get out of here," said Cosmo. And he and Sammy took off down the wharf with the gang shoving after them through the crowd.

"Don't let 'em go under the wharf or we'll never catch 'em," shouted the redhead, huffing and puffing at the rear of the chase.

Feeling the gang gaining on him, Sammy ran as hard as he could. It was an all-out dash and his short legs churned like

propellers on an outboard engine. Still, he couldn't keep up
with his brother. Cosmo had sped so far ahead that his yellow
shirt was just a bright blur in the distance.

Two of the fastest gang boys were now right on Sammy's
heels. Their galloping feet rumbled the planks beneath him,
deadening his stride and turning his legs to spaghetti. Sammy
knew he'd never make it to the end of the wharf.

Cosmo, looking back, also must have realized it. He stopped
in front of the Monterey Fish Company and yelled to Sammy,
"This way, quick!" Then he ducked behind a sputtering
forklift, ran up a row of fish crates stacked stair-like beside
the building, and leaped to the balcony of the art gallery next
door.

Seeing this, Sammy picked up speed. In a matter of seconds he, too, came tearing around the forklift, which suddenly backed up with a roar of black exhaust and cut off his
two pursuers. Sammy didn't look back, but bounded up the
crates to the balcony.

"Where now?" he asked, breathing hard.

"Up here," said Cosmo, who was standing on the rail of the
balcony and testing the strength of the rain gutter. Satisfied,
he pulled himself onto the roof and out of sight. A moment
later he peeked back over the edge and yelled, "Come on!"

Sammy sprang up and mounted the railing. With Cosmo
tugging from above, he soon clawed and kicked his way onto
the roof. It was flat and covered with green tar paper dappled
with pigeon dung. Sammy's hands and clothes were messy
with the stuff by the time he rolled to his feet.

Feeling lost and dizzy, Sammy scanned the long row of
rooftops looking for a familiar landmark. Nothing seemed the
same. Wires shrouded the horizon like rigging. The roofs
pitched and peaked in all angles and directions. Tin chimneys
and rusted flue pipes sprouted like mushrooms out of the

mossy shingles and warped tar paper. Weathered signboards stared backward blankly. And strewn atop the various buildings were cracked basins, empty cans, an old ladder and other rubbish.

It disturbed Sammy to see that the wharf he thought he knew so well was actually quite different when viewed from this new level in the glaring light of day. He much preferred its dark, shadowy underside.

"There's no way down," said Cosmo, returning from his survey along the roof's edge. "We'll have to jump to the next building."

Sammy followed his brother to the jumping-off point and peered over the edge. Luckily, the flat gravel roof of the barroom next door was a bit lower than the art gallery's, and the gap of air in between was only a few feet wide. All that separated the two buildings was a narrow plank and some gas meters. But those were two stories down.

"You first," said Sammy.

"All right, but don't chicken out," Cosmo warned. "There's no telling what they'll do if they catch you."

Cosmo backed up from the edge, took a running leap, and sailed gracefully through the air. He landed squarely on the other roof, kicking up gravel and jolting the bag of firecrackers out of his pocket. Then he turned and shouted to Sammy, "Hurry up, they're coming!"

Glancing back, Sammy froze with panic at the sight of the two guys climbing up to the roof. Despite Cosmo's example, Sammy hadn't decided whether to jump or not. But now there was no choice. He measured his steps back toward the center of the building. Then, just as one of the gang kids took off after him, Sammy sprinted for the edge. He reached it going full speed and, with arms and legs still pumping, flew over the abyss and smacked down onto the barroom roof. His pursuer managed to stop just before falling over, and Cosmo pelted him with gravel.

Meantime, the redhead and his other stooges had scaled the gallery and were now advancing toward the edge.

"Give me those firecrackers," he demanded.

Cosmo answered with another fistful of gravel. Then he asked, "Do you really want them?"

"You know I do," snarled the redhead. "They're mine."

"Well, then go get them," said Cosmo as he scooped up the bag and hurled it over the back of the building. The sack spun end-over-end, spilling its stock of firecrackers, skyrockets, and cherry bombs, all of which plopped into the bay.

"You've ruined them!" screamed the redhead. "You've ruined them all! I swear I'll make you pay!"

"Let's keep going," whispered Cosmo to Sammy. "If we can make that jump, so can they."

The two brothers hurried to the far side of the roof, stepping carefully through the debris. At the edge they saw there was a sheer drop, with no drain pipes, window ledges or footholds of any kind. Stored down in the alley were some trash cans and cases of empty beer bottles. But these were too low to be of any help.

On the other side of the alley, some six feet away, loomed the blackened packing house. Gutted by fire long ago, its windows were now boarded up and the entire structure leaned askew. The roof sloped steeply and Sammy could see the scorched rafters running up near the ridge where the shingles were missing. KEEP OUT signs were posted on the two side doors. But as Sammy studied the building he decided its rickety staircase provided the perfect escape route, if only he and Cosmo could reach its overhang.

Sammy looked back and saw the redhead standing on a metal air duct and motioning his minions to jump. None of them seemed overeager to obey the petty tyrant. Then Sammy spotted the old ladder he had just stepped over. "That's the thing!" he said, and ran over and dragged it back to Cosmo.

"Here," said Sammy. "What if we lean this across and crawl to that little roof over the stairs?"

Cosmo eyed the ladder skeptically. It was weathered and bowed, and a few of its rungs were cracked or missing. But on jostling it, he felt that it was still pretty sturdy. Looking back at the overhang, he said, "Let's try it."

They stood the ladder up at the edge and, holding firmly onto the bottom, let the top end fall across the void. The ladder was right on target, but it bounced so sharply against the overhang that it stung the boys' hands like a zap of electricity.

"You first," said Cosmo. "I'll hold on."

Sammy shook out the buzzing in his hands and crawled onto the makeshift bridge. He advanced slowly up the slight incline, ignoring the pain it put on his knees.

"Don't look down," advised Cosmo from behind.

Sammy hadn't been tempted before, but now he couldn't resist peering through the rungs. It was a big mistake, for the alley seemed to take off in a spin miles below him. Sammy stopped and clung to the ladder.

"You're almost there!" urged Cosmo.

Forcing himself to focus on the roof, Sammy started crawling again. The instant his hand touched the overhang he scrambled onto it, kicking the ladder a bit out of place in his hurry. He made sure, though, to keep his body low against the roof, which felt much steeper than it looked.

"Okay," said Sammy. "I'll hold it now."

Cosmo looked back and saw the gang watching him and Sammy in awe. None of them had even attempted the jump yet. Cosmo then kneeled lightly on the ladder, testing its flex, and crawled forward. His every move was smooth and balanced, but midway out the ladder skidded in the gravel and jerked to one side.

"It's sliding!" screamed Sammy.

Cosmo lunged forward, reached past Sammy, and grabbed onto a shingle just as the ladder crashed down. An explosion of breaking bottles and banging garbage cans reverberated up from the alley. Cosmo's legs dangled dangerously over the roof's edge.

"Give me some room," he said.

"I can't," cried Sammy. "You've got me pinned."

Cosmo tried to swing his legs up but the motion wrenched the shingle out of the roof and he slid farther over the edge. Cosmo dug his nails into the other shingles, but the wood just splintered and bloodied his fingers with each inch lost. At the last second he grabbed Sammy's legs. Sammy clung to Cosmo's shirt and leaned back as far as he could, but he now felt himself being tugged toward the edge.

"We're gonna fall!" he cried.

Cosmo felt it too and looked up at Sammy, who saw fear for the first time in his brother's eyes. They slipped some more and Cosmo flashed a sad, weak smile. Then he let go.

"Hold on!" screamed Sammy.

But there was a great rip and Cosmo plummeted downward. His body slammed against an overturned trash can, denting it, and rolled in a crumpled heap faceup in the alley.

"No, no, no," sobbed Sammy, still gripping a piece of Cosmo's T-shirt. Sammy looked around desperately for help and started to call out to the gang boys. But through his tears he could see them running away.

Sammy looked down again at his brother. Cosmo's eyes were still open, but crimson blood trickled from his mouth,

his nose, his ears. Sammy knew it was Cosmo's life ebbing away. There was no way of cheating it, of pretending he hadn't noticed.

"I'm sorry," cried Sammy. "I'm sorry."

Cosmo just lay there motionless, his lifeless eyes staring blankly, like the statue's.

CHAPTER FOUR
Marooned

RATZO'S WIFE bustled around Aunt Nastina's kitchen, setting out cakes, salads, cold cuts and french bread. Coffee popped and burbled in the big percolator she had brought and its sharp smell filled the flat. Taking off her apron, she went into the front room and saw Sammy still slumped miserably in one of the straight-backed chairs lining the wall. His face was pale and eyes downcast. His hair had been slicked back and he was dressed in a new button-down shirt, bow tie, and the kind of gray slacks that itch.

"You look very nice today," she said.

Sammy didn't respond, but gazed absently at his pointy black dress shoes hanging crossed above the floor. They were once Cosmo's, and Sammy was thinking how his brother had complained about their pinch and style so intently that Aunt Nastina finally closed her ears and made him wear the shoes to church one Easter, even after he had outgrown them by two sizes.

"I know it's hard," Ratzo's wife went on, "but everyone will be back soon. Try to show them how brave you are."

Brave-shmave, thought Sammy. What difference does it make? They don't care. They don't know what it's like. . . . Cosmo's fall flashed through his mind again, as it had done hundreds of times over the last few days. It haunted his imagination like a shark in the murky waters of its favorite feeding ground. And every time it surfaced Sammy felt his insides being devoured, leaving a black hole of terror and loss.

He had first felt that emptiness when Sergeant Abner climbed up the creaking stairs of the condemned packing house and lifted him off the overhang. A crowd had gathered below, but their frantic shouts had turned to murmurs. Someone had thrown a white tablecloth over Cosmo's body, into which circles of blood slowly soaked. A siren neared and an ambulance soon pulled up, its red light flashing. Two men in white jumped out and knelt over Cosmo for a minute, and then calmly lifted him onto a stretcher and into the rear door of the ambulance. Aunt Nastina arrived now, screaming hysterically. She pounded on the ambulance until the men let her in. After they sped away, Sergeant Abner carried Sammy back to the flat and laid him on the couch in the front room, telling him to rest until someone came. Late that night Sammy heard knocks at the door and moments later saw a dark figure standing over him. It was Ratzo's wife. She cried while putting him to bed and sat up stroking his head. "He's with Mama now," she kept saying. "He's with Mama and Papa." Sammy just stared into the darkness.

The next day Sergeant Abner came back and took Sammy to his booth. He asked him questions over and over again. How did they get on the roof? What were they doing? Who else was up there? A jumble of answers ran through Sammy's mind, but he couldn't speak. Where would he begin? With that stupid redhead killing seagulls on the beach? It was all his fault! He's the one! He should have been killed, thought Sammy. And he envisioned himself rescuing Cosmo from the gang and beating the redhead with an oar.

But then something drained him of this rage, something

deeper, more disturbing, and impossible to put into words; impossible because just the thought paralyzed him. Deep down Sammy knew that the redhead wasn't to blame, but that it was his own fault. It had been his lousy idea to use the ladder and he had knocked it crooked. He had killed Cosmo! And now he was alone, marooned forever in a brotherless world.

Sammy suddenly heard footsteps on the back stairs and a knock at the door. He looked up and saw Ratzo peek in. "We're back," he called. Ratzo flung open the door and walked in. He was nattily decked out in a pin-striped suit, and Sammy realized it was the first time he had seen him out of his rubber boots and apron. Behind Ratzo came Babe, Angelo, his brothers, and other wharf merchants and fishermen. Some carried flowers or foil-covered casseroles.

"Here, let me take those," said Ratzo's wife. "How did everything go?"

"It turned out nice," said Ratzo, "short and sweet. How's the boy?" He went over and patted Sammy's cheek. "Feeling better? Good, good. We gotta look ahead. That's the only way. What's past is past."

The others walked in talking excitedly, but on seeing Sammy their tone dropped and the cheer left their voices. Then Aunt Nastina entered, looking rather elegant in her long black coat, gloves and veiled hat. They contrasted sharply against her pale skin and blue-tinted hair. She noticed all the food in the kitchen as Ratzo helped her off with her coat.

"Oh, how lovely," she said. "You're all so kind. Thank you. Thank you. Go ahead and start, you must be famished. It was such a long ceremony. Monsignor O'Casey does tend to go on." She looked at Sammy and saw him in the same position as when she left. "You haven't moved an inch, have you?

Well, I'm not surprised. I knew it was better you stayed home. Funerals can be so traumatic."

Turning back to her guests, she said, "But the parlor did a nice job on Cosmo, no?" Everyone nodded in agreement. "Last night at the rosary he looked just like he was sleeping. So peaceful! I didn't want an open casket at first—what with the head injuries. But they did a nice job. That white tuxedo was beautiful; made him look like a little groom. A little sleeping groom.

"And do you know who was there today?" she asked Sammy. "The mayor! Imagine, the mayor of Monterey at your brother's funeral! It was an honor. He didn't have to come, you know."

Sammy imagined the mayor looking down at Cosmo in the casket. Then their images slowly reversed and Cosmo was standing over the embalmed mayor. Sammy realized his mind was playing tricks on him and he shook the picture out of his head.

Aunt Nastina stopped her nervous monologue and all eyes were on Sammy. Slumped in the shell of his seat, he looked as lonesome as a hermit crab. He wasn't crying or carrying on, yet everyone knew he was grieving in a much deeper way. Some commented on his condition as they began to fill their plates.

"It's too much for him," whispered Babe to Angelo. "First his parents and now his brother. A grown man can't hardly take that much loss; no telling how it could affect a boy."

Sammy heard them talking and caught their sympathetic glances, but he read them as looks of blame. He knew they secretly held him responsible for Cosmo's death. He just knew it! They wouldn't admit it, of course. No one told the truth about anything anymore. Sammy wished they'd all just leave.

At that moment Jenko came through the door accompanied

by his two actress friends. They, too, were dressed in black. The actresses guided Jenko past Aunt Nastina, who jumped back as if his blindness were contagious. They sat Jenko down in the chair beside Sammy and then leaned over and kissed his cheek.

"We're so sorry," said the one who had played the queen.

"Yes, Sammy, and I'm sorry you weren't at the funeral," said Jenko. "I was looking for you." He smiled like he always did when he made dumb jokes about his blindness. "Really," he said, "most are a bit too grim for my taste, but at least they're something. So how are you?"

Sammy didn't feel like talking and was going to just shrug. But since Jenko wouldn't be able to see it, he weakly uttered his first words since the fall: "I dunno."

"Hungry?" asked Jenko. "Something smells good. Maybe the girls wouldn't mind making us a plate."

"Of course not," said the one who had played the Indian, and they both left for the kitchen.

"Listen, Sammy," said Jenko, leaning close and cradling the boy's neck with his big hand. "Your head must be swirling with the worst kind of confusion. If you need someone to talk to later on, you know where I am. Come anytime. I mean it."

Animated greetings suddenly rippled through the group standing out on the porch. "Hey, hey!" "Look who's here!" "What d'ya know?" In walked Benny the organ grinder holding Buffa on his hip like a baby. Both were dressed like colorful Italian peasants, and Benny's mustache was waxed into wonderfully long handlebars.

"'Ello, 'ello, 'ello," said Benny as he made his way toward Sammy. He tipped his feathered felt hat to everyone. Then he crumpled it against his heart and very seriously told Sammy, "Sorry innarupt da party, but Buffa an' me—we joost wanna come by before work anna pay our respect. Is okay?"

Sammy nodded.

"We you friends—*tre amici,* huh? If you need ennat'ing, joost you ask. Here, dis from Buffa."

Benny placed a bag of saltwater taffy in Sammy's hand. Buffa then climbed out of Benny's arms and into Sammy's lap. The monkey chattered away at Sammy, presumably offering condolences in her own language. Although Sammy usually was overjoyed at a chance to hold her, today he leaned away.

"Please, Benny!" hollered Aunt Nastina. "Can't you see the boy is upset? You'll have to take that animal out." She marched up and pointed to the door.

Buffa quickly leaped from Sammy's lap onto Aunt Nastina's outstretched arm. She swung as if on a branch and let loose with a stream of monkey talk. Aunt Nastina screamed and pulled back, but Buffa hung on.

"Get this beast . . . " Before she could finish her sentence, Buffa planted one of her famous kisses on Aunt Nastina's lips and jumped back into Benny's arms. Nastina screamed again and started spitting and slapping imaginary germs out of her mouth.

"*Ciao,*" said Benny as he headed for the door with Buffa securely in tow.

"Good-bye!" shouted Aunt Nastina, who then stomped into the bathroom.

Everybody was laughing and Sammy sighed a crooked smile that turned instantly to a cringe. He hurt and didn't want anything to do with silliness. He just wanted to be by himself. But the actresses appeared now and handed him and Jenko each a plate. Jenko dug into his, but Sammy just held his along with the bag of candy.

Benny was right, he thought. This is nothing but a big party. Cosmo dies and everyone comes over to eat and drink and celebrate. Sammy didn't understand it. He wished he could just go to his room and shut the door. But people were up there now looking at the view. Then he remembered the only place he could really be alone—the secret shed.

"That monkey will never set foot in here again," vowed Aunt Nastina as she came out of the bathroom. "He causes more mischief than Cosmo used to."

"I don't know about that," said Ratzo, setting down his plate and leaning back on the couch. "He and Sammy were like hard bread and a dull knife—nothing but trouble together. Why, I remember the first day they got here. One minute they were nosing around my dock and the next Cosmo's yelling 'Sammy fell in! Sammy fell in!' I run out back and see nothing but bubbles coming up. Naturally, I think the kid's drowning. So I pull off my boots and am about to jump in—me who swims like a cement block—when little Sammy—he was practically a baby then—comes out from behind the winch. That Cosmo had thrown a pop bottle in the water! I let him have it good that time, poor guy."

"He was a character, all right," said Babe. "Remember last year when he went around asking everyone for work? How could you say no?"

"Easy," said Angelo.

"For a tightwad like you, maybe. But me, I paid him to wash down the boat. No harm, right? Next thing I hear he's going to union meetings and beefing about low wages. Claimed he was working for peanuts—like Buffa."

Everyone laughed.

"That's nothing," said Angelo. "Just this summer he sold me twenty pounds of clams that. . . . "

One by one, they reminisced about Cosmo. Sammy listened, surprised that the things which had gotten them into so much trouble were now just funny stories. But the stories seemed to bring Cosmo back to life, and Sammy found it hard to believe that he was really dead, that he wouldn't be the next one to come through the door.

After a while Aunt Nastina suggested that Sammy go take a nap. "Too much excitement for one day," she said, and ordered everyone out of his room.

"See ya, Sammy." "So long now." "Get some rest," said the guests as they watched him trudge solemnly up the stairs.

Alone in his room, Sammy took off his shirt and tie and itchy pants and hung them on the door knob. He could hear everyone talking again as he got his pajamas out from under his pillow and put them on. He looked at Cosmo's empty bed and felt his throat tighten and tears slide down his cheeks. He went over and got into it. Finding Cosmo's pajamas under the pillow, he pressed them to his face and inhaled the lingering smell of his brother. Sammy cried now, violent sobs which he tried painfully to smother.

Long after all the guests had left, Sammy fell into a deep gunnysack of sleep where he tossed and turned for what seemed like an eternity. In the middle of the night, however, he was awakened by the bump of boats against the pilings and the whistling of wind through timbers. It went Woooooh . . . Woooooh. . . . and Sammy knew it was that cursed packing house.

Unable to lie there in the dark any longer, he got up and went to the closet. He pulled his jeans over his pajamas, threw on his green sweatshirt, and wriggled into his sneakers. Then he quietly opened the window behind Cosmo's bed and climbed out into the cold, foggy night.

Way off on China Point, the foghorn heaved a forbidding belch. Sammy looked up, half expecting to see the sound rolling in like a wave. Yet all he saw was a pale crescent moon, a mere thumbnail clip waxing dim through the spitting mist.

He walked on, fists thrust deep in his sweatshirt pocket and shoulders arched up to keep the damp air off his neck. He hadn't been outside since the day of the fall and the chill felt good against his face.

Sammy passed the washed-down markets and padlocked bars. He came upon a bent beer can and began kicking it—sklankety-dank—down the wharf. Fog hovered yellow around the wharf lamps. The horn sounded again in the distance.

Catching his reflection in a restaurant window, Sammy stopped. He looked strange and evil to himself, like a criminal. Garbage cans were lined up below the window and their stink suddenly hit him. Moisture dripped from the eaves, dinking the lids and glossing the uncovered trash.

He heard a rustling and saw something stir in the shadows. It looked like a big cat, maybe two. No! Digging through the spilled garbage were two huge rats, gray as grime, with thick, pinkish tails over a foot long. Sammy's heart pounded as he eased down to pick up the can—his only hope for a weapon. The rats looked up, eyed him with indifference, and continued foraging.

Sammy shivered and hurried on. He never knew how big and brazen rats could be. He hadn't seen any before, not even under the wharf. But now he felt sure the filthy rodents had been there all along, waiting to pounce hungrily on his bare neck and tear into his flesh.

Sammy was still shaken when he reached the old packing house. It rose with a crippled tilt higher than the other buildings and darker than the dark sky. A light wind blew in through the charred roof and wheezed out through the boarded doors and windows, making that eerie, taunting sound, Woooooh . . . Woooooh. . . . The alley beside the packing house, where Cosmo had died, was nothing but a tunnel of blackness.

"You don't belong here!" shouted Sammy. "They shoulda tore you down a long time ago." He threw the can as hard as he could at the building, but it fell short. He had only managed to spray himself with stale beer.

Sammy scuffed on to the wharf's end, his clothes heavy with dampness. Standing right at the edge, he watched the fog waft thinly overhead. It turned the closely-moored boats into formless spectres and swallowed up the entire bay beyond. The foghorn blasted another warning and Sammy jumped back. He felt that same gnawing emptiness in his belly and realized that one day he too would die, he too would be swallowed by eternity.

Sammy shivered once more and spun around for home. But the narrow, fog-drenched pier now seemed sabotaged; its crooked cardlike buildings set to collapse upon anyone who walked between them. He forced himself onward, eyes darting right and left. Then he noticed the light in Jenko's upstairs window.

The old sculptor was sitting on a stool in the center of his studio chiseling a bust-shaped block of marble braced on sawhorses. He was cast in the light of a metal-shaded bulb hanging above him on a cord. It was the only light in the vast, otherwise blackened studio.

Jenko's beard, apron, and the floor around him were dusted white with chips and powder from the marble. Even his black high-top tennis shoes were now white. Sweat glistened on Jenko's forehead and his shining eyes betrayed an intense concentration that had nothing to do with sight. He rubbed the gouge he had just cut and then made another, striking the chisel squarely with the mallet. The sound of steel against stone rang through the cavernous studio.

Pausing again to stroke his work, Jenko heard someone at the top of the stairs. "Who's there?" he shouted in a voice that rousted the pigeons sleeping in the rafters.

"It's me," answered Sammy.

"Hmmm, I thought I heard someone out there. Up pretty late, aren't you? Couldn't you sleep?"

"I didn't want to."

Jenko nodded. "I know how it is. Happens to me more and more. It's true what they say—the older you get, the less you sleep. But what are you, nine? Ten? Too young to be town crier. I'm sorry. All's not well, is it? Come over here where I can see you?"

Sammy walked carefully down the dark aisle between two shelves and entered the circle of light. The brightness hurt his eyes. "Why do you have that light on, anyway?" he asked.

"Oh, just a courtesy for late-night visitors such as yourself. And so folks won't think the place is haunted if they hear me rattling around."

Sammy looked down and saw powder settling on his own sneakers. Then he said, "You know what's really haunted? That old packing house Cosmo fell off of. Someone should tear it down."

"You may be right, Sammy. That place has had a bad history. I wouldn't be surprised if it is razed soon."

"I said it should be torn down, not raised up!"

"I know. I heard you. I meant razed with a 'z.' It sounds the same as the other raise but means the opposite. Some words are tricky that way."

"Raze-shmaze, all I know is that Coz would still be here if it wasn't for that building."

"You know, Sammy, I don't think there's much point in trying to lay the blame somewhere."

"Well, it's not my fault!" he shouted.

"No, of course not," said Jenko in a worried tone. After an uneasy silence, he added, "You don't mind if I keep working while we talk, do you?"

"I don't care," said Sammy, shifting his weight from one leg to the other, his hands still tucked in his pockets.

Jenko began chiseling again. His sleeves were rolled up and Sammy noticed the veins bulging in his hairy forearms. His gnarled fists held the tools firmly, yet he chipped away delicately, lovingly, caressing the stone after each chip.

Sammy had always wondered how Jenko had gone blind, and he was about to ask but then changed his mind. "What are you making?" he asked instead.

"It's my pet project," said Jenko, smiling. "A bust of myself. What do you think?"

"It's not finished."

Jenko laughed. "Well, that's a fair observation. But it feels right so far, and that's the main thing. No one to please but myself on this one. I've had it with commissioned work for a while. Did you hear what happened to the Columbus statue?"

"No."

"Well, first off, that spineless bunch on the town council rejected it—with the mayor's recommendation, of course. 'Not consistent with the terms of the agreement,' they said. Nitpicking ninnies! Normally I wouldn't even care, but when I asked that the piece be returned they told me they couldn't, that it was missing."

"Missing? What do you mean 'missing'?"

"I mean gone. Stolen! Swiped! Kidnapped! I don't know. I can't understand it either. Maybe someone wanted it for firewood. Dirty crooks! Cosmo and I put in a lot of hours on that one. He was proud of it too. The council should have accepted it, if only to honor his memory. I bet it wouldn't have been stolen then."

"Why did he have to die, Jenko?"

The sculptor's face softened. "Geez, Sammy. I'm sorry. Here I am carrying on about a piece of wood. I am sorry." He paused and thought for a moment. "I don't know what to tell you. It's just something that happens to us all at one time or another. I know it seems unfair. And it is. It's terrible. But you have to hope that it's not really the end; that it's the beginning of something new. You know, the opposite of what it seems."

"It's the end all right," said Sammy. "Cosmo's gone and it's the end of everything."

Jenko sighed and chiseled some more. "You're right," he said finally. "But I think there are two kinds of ends. Look here at what I'm doing. The end of my sculpting is when I make the last cut." Jenko struck the chisel and a chip flew off. "But the end is also to create a bust of myself. So you see, it can be both the finish and the purpose. Try to look at his death that way."

"I don't get it."

"I'm just saying that what seems like a cruel blow may actually be part of some wonderful master plan. It's a matter of perspective, of where you're looking from."

"I still don't get it."

"Let me put it this way. Have you ever watched the tide take something away from shore, say a bottle or a piece of driftwood?"

Sammy thought back and saw the seagull's carcass being washed out to sea. "Yeah," he said. "So what?"

"Well, if *you* were the bottle or the driftwood, it might feel like you were taking the tide."

"What's the difference?"

"Perspective!" said Jenko, jabbing his finger in the air.

Sammy shrugged and Jenko resumed sculpting. After a while, he said, "You know, Sammy, dying is a challenge we all have to face sometime. We both know that Cosmo loved challenges. He loved adventure. Now he's on the greatest one of all."

"I wish we both fell," said Sammy.

"Nah," said Jenko, shaking his head. "Life is good too, and you've got a lot of it ahead of you—things to do, places to go, people to see!"

"I hate it here now. I hate it without him. I wish we never came to this wharf." Sammy turned to leave.

"Scaring you away with all my crazy double-talk, huh? Wait a minute. Where are you going?"

"Nowhere," said Sammy, now clutching the handrail and peering down the dark stairwell.

"There's something you're forgetting," yelled Jenko.

"What?"

"Remember that skiff you brought over here? It's still on the dock out back. Cosmo'd be sorry if you didn't follow through on it."

"I don't want it anymore."

"Well, neither do I. You'd better do something with it, one way or . . . "

Galloping down the stairs, Sammy didn't hear Jenko finish. He had already made up his mind to go to the shed and never, ever come out again.

CHAPTER FIVE
Whispers Under The Wharf

SAMMY, GET UP. I want you to help me in the shop today."
Aunt Nastina, already dressed and made up for work, was
standing at the foot of the stairs. "Sammy, answer me!" She
listened for a sleepy groan but heard nothing. Grumbling, she
climbed the stairs.

As she opened the door, Sammy's dress clothes slid off the
knob. She saw at once that he was gone. The window was
open and his bed hadn't been slept in. Yet Cosmo's was an
unmade mess. "That's strange," she said.

She picked up Sammy's clothes and brought them to the
closet, where she noticed that his sneakers were missing and
his favorite sweatshirt wasn't on its hook. She frowned,
resenting the worry that shot through her.

On her way to reopen the shop for the first time since
Cosmo's death, Aunt Nastina made a detour to Sergeant
Abner's booth. She found him sitting outside it on a padded
barrel donated by Angelo. He was in full uniform, with his
blue policeman's cap perched casually on the back of his
head. A yellow pencil poked out of the white hair around his
ears, and on his lap was a clipboard half filled with the
license numbers of the vehicles already on the wharf.

"Abner, have you seen Sammy?" demanded Aunt Nastina
as she approached his station.

He spun to face her. "Good morning, Agnestina. No, no I haven't. What's wrong?"

"He's disappeared. He wasn't in his room when I got up this morning."

"Well, he's probably around here somewhere."

"Abner, he hasn't left the house since the accident. And you know how strange he's been acting. Last night he even slept in his brother's bed."

"So?"

"So can't you look for him? What *do* I pay taxes for?"

"Okay, okay. I'll ask around."

An hour later Sergeant Abner climbed down from his barrel and reached in through the booth's Dutch door to fish out his ticket book. He hiked up his holster and then set off on his rounds, looking forward to the meal he always had along the way.

But first he went over to where Benny was unrolling his carpet. Buffa, tied to the railing by her leash, was chomping on an onion, her favorite snack.

"Getting ready for a big day?" asked Sergeant Abner.

Benny looked up, surprised, then smiled. "No, gonna be slow again. But whatcha gonna do?"

"Say, you haven't seen little Sammy around, have you?"

"No, we joost come here. Whatsa matta?"

"I don't know. Agnestina says he's missing."

"You t'inking he inna trob?"

"Too soon to tell. Keep your eyes open, though, huh?"

"Okay," said Benny.

Sergeant Abner flicked the brim of his cap in salute and continued on.

Only a few tourists were on the wharf now and most of the merchants were preparing for the day ahead. Shopkeepers swept their entryways, cooks peeled onions and potatoes out open doors, and delivery men carted bread, linen, and other supplies to and from their trucks.

Sergeant Abner stopped and chatted with nearly everyone, always remembering to ask about Sammy. He asked Babe, whose shiny boat was in a harness and about to be winched back into the water. He asked Ratzo, who was sticking pronged price tags into the fillets on display in his market. And he even asked old Gao, who was trotting bowlegged off the wharf, the baskets of his shoulder pole filled with fish.

But no one had seen the boy.

Sergeant Abner also stopped in front of Angelo's Restaurant, where Angelo's white Cadillac was parked. The officer checked his watch, then his clipboard, and shook his head in disappointment. He was writing up a ticket when Angelo flew out the door.

"I'm gone already, Abner. I'm moving it right now."

"Sorry, Ange. You've been two hours in a twenty-minute zone."

"Abner, I had two waitresses and a bartender call in sick. I've been on the phone all morning. Gimme a break."

"I don't know, Ange."

"Come on, I'm outa here now. Go into the bar and order yourself some lunch. I'll join you in a minute."

Abner checked his watch again. It was almost twelve. An abalone sandwich might be just the thing to keep up his strength on the job, he decided, and flipped his ticket book shut.

After lunch, while ambling back up the wharf, Sergeant Abner passed the two actresses. They were now wearing the latest fashion—bobby sox, tweed skirts and sweaters. "Hello, ladies," he said. "Matinee today?"

"Yes. When are you going to come see us?" said the once-reigning queen.

"Oh, one of these day," said Abner, who hated plays. "Listen, you don't happen to know where the Serafino kid is, do you?"

"You mean Sammy? No. Have you asked Jenko?"

"Not yet. Good idea. By the way, how is he taking the news about his sculpture?"

"I don't know," said the former Indian over her shoulder. "But I think it's awful."

Inside the Lighthouse Gift Shop, Aunt Nastina was guarding the cash register and watching her young assistant dust shelves when Sergeant Abner walked in. "Hi there," he said. "Did Sammy show up for lunch?"

"It's about time," complained Aunt Nastina. "No, I was just upstairs. He hasn't been back. He's doing this to spite me, you know."

"Hold on, Agnestina. He could be with Jenko. Why don't you go pay him a visit?"

"That deadbeat!"

"Come on," urged Abner. "You may not like him anymore, but he has been close to the kids."

Aunt Nastina looked around at the few browsing customers. "Okay," she said, "but you come with me. Sarah, watch the shop."

The burly, bare-chested sculptor was sitting up in bed running his fingertips over a large braille library book when he heard visitors in his studio. He stopped reading, and instantly regretted having stayed in bed so late. He was about to spring up and throw on a robe when he heard a knock. From behind the curtain came Sergeant Abner's voice.

"Jenko, it's me, Abner. Are you up?"

Jenko's face lit up. "Abner, what is it? Have you found my Columbus?"

Aunt Nastina swept the curtain aside and burst into the room. She froze, seeing Jenko's big, hairy chest rising out of the blankets.

"My God!" she exclaimed. "Couldn't you cover yourself?"

"Agnestina! You too?" said Jenko. "It's been so long."

"Not long enough," she said. "Please put something on."

"So sorry to shock you," laughed Jenko, "but you haven't seen anything yet." Raising his arms, he flexed his chest muscles so that they jerked and bobbed like two sailors doing a jig.

"Do you mind?" asked Aunt Nastina sternly.

"Sorry to barge in on you, Jenko," said Sergeant Abner as he stepped across the threshold, "but we have a problem. Sammy's missing. I thought maybe you might have seen him. I mean, that he might have come around. Has he?"

"Well, well," said Jenko, relaxing his torso. "As a matter of fact he was here last night, rather late. Said he couldn't sleep."

"Any idea where he went?" asked Sergeant Abner.

"No," said Jenko.

Abner took out a note pad and grabbed the pencil behind his ear. "What time was it exactly?" he asked.

"Oh, I don't know. What time is it now?" Jenko leaned over toward the nightstand and felt the hands on his crystal-less clock. "Hmmm, I'd say it was around 3 a.m."

"What on earth was he doing here at that hour?" asked Aunt Nastina.

"He just wanted to talk, I guess. Too bad I wasn't much help. He left worse off than he came."

"What do you mean?" asked Sergeant Abner.

"Well, he was saying how he wished he had fallen along with Cosmo. That kind of thing."

"Why didn't you bring him back home?" shouted Aunt Nastina. "You know the condition he's in."

"What condition? The kid's mourning. You can't stop that."

"I'm very disappointed in you, Jenko," Aunt Nastina lamented falsely. "I would have hoped that for once you could have acted responsibly."

"Tina, do you mean you really still had hopes for me?" said Jenko, clutching his heart tenderly.

"You haven't changed a bit," she snapped back. "You always were a failure and you always will be!"

"And you always were a sweet-talker. Why don't you just go back to that junk store of yours and wait for the kid to come back when he misses your delightful company."

"Junk store! Just because I wouldn't carry your overpriced whittlings . . ."

"All right, all right. Cut it out, you two," interrupted Abner.

"Sergeant, arrest that man!" cried Aunt Nastina.

"For what?" he asked.

"Criminal negligence. Indecent exposure. Anything!"

"Sorry," replied Sergeant Abner. "There's only one thing to do now."

"What?" asked Jenko and Nastina together.

"Send out a search party."

The sun, like a scoop of orange sherbet, was now melting into the horizon and still no one had found a trace of Sammy.

Sergeant Abner had passed the word and enlisted scores of local folks into the search. He split them into groups, which combed the shoreline north and south. They also hunted high and low on the wharf, checking every ledge, dock and alleyway.

Abner dispatched some of Ratzo's crew to scan the rooftops, and directed Babe, Benny and Buffa to look under the wharf.

Theirs was the dirtiest of jobs, but Buffa enjoyed it immensely. She scampered across the planks and swung from pipe to pipe as if she were back in the jungle of her ancestors. Benny, however, crawled along nervously on his hands and knees. His once colorful peasant costume was now splotched with piling tar and soiled worse than if he had actually labored a season in the vineyards of Italy.

The poor organ grinder's head throbbed from having bumped it repeatedly on the beams. And his hair was full of cobwebs. To make matters worse, a large, whiskered sea lion lolled and snorted in the water below him. It was a harmless old sport, but when Benny heard its plank-rattling bark and looked down at its huge white teeth and pink throat, he thought for sure it was waiting for him to fall.

"Dear San Vito," he prayed. "Call da sea line; 'e wanna eat me."

Benny did not fall, but the sun did. And as it grew darker he considered turning back. "Buffa, *Vene ca!* Come here, is getting late," he called. But the monkey darted back and forth, caught up in the excitement of the hunt. He clearly understood the purpose of their expedition, but neither of them could find a clue as to Sammy's whereabouts since they were nowhere near his secret shed.

Babe, on the other hand, was quite close. He had bumped his head once too often while following Buffa and returned to his skiff, which hung on pulleys near the end of the wharf. Having lowered it into the water, he was now standing up pushing it through the pilings, guided by the light of a lantern in the bow. Every so often he'd call out Sammy's name.

Meanwhile, safe in his shed, Sammy sat watching the candle flicker on the table and shadows dance on the walls. He hadn't slept at all and was groggy and hungry, but still resolved to stay there by himself.

He could tell by the idling engines, footsteps and other sounds coming through the planks that it had been a normal day up on the wharf. It occurred to him that life was going on without him, just as it was going on without Cosmo.

He looked over at the picture of his parents by the sailboat. At one time he thought he remembered the day it was taken, but now he wasn't sure if the memory had merely grown out of the photo and his desire to remember.

Sammy gradually became aware of an unusual echoing, a deep, melodious cry that rose and fell in the distance: "Saaa-meee . . . Saaa-meee. . . . "

He got up and peeked out the door. At first he didn't see anyone, but then there was a flash between the pilings four or five rows away. A man in a strangely lighted skiff was drifting toward the shed.

Sammy ducked back inside and propped the door shut with the coffee can. He was about to blow out the candle when a voice behind him said, "Relax. No one will find you here."

Sammy's skin rippled numb when he heard the voice. He stood dead still, holding the breath that would have blown out the candle. Even his suspicions froze half-formed in his head. Then he spun around to face the intruder. What he saw made him stagger backwards, as if smacked by an icy breaker.

There in the corner, sprawled out on the pile of nets, was a bleary figure that could only be Cosmo. He was grinning his cocky grin and wearing the same white tuxedo he was buried in. Yet he was barefoot, and with legs stretched out and hands pillowed behind his head, he looked like a millionaire on holiday.

Sammy rubbed his eyes.

"It's me all right," said Cosmo. "Didn't you know I'd come back?"

"I . . . I don't believe it," said Sammy. "How could it be?"

"Easy," said Cosmo.

Sammy pressed forward and squinted, expecting the vision to disappear. Cosmo's outline and features swam in a vapor, but candlelight shone clearly in his dark eyes.

"Are you real?" demanded Sammy.

"More real than ever," replied Cosmo.

"Oh, I knew it! I knew you couldn't just die." And Sammy made a diving tackle onto his brother. But his body passed right through Cosmo's and he tumbled onto the net.

"Relax," said Cosmo, getting up to sit at the table. "I never said I didn't die. That fall did me in. I'm a ghost."

"A ghost!" gasped Sammy.

Cosmo nodded and Sammy fell back, confused and dejected.

"It takes some getting used to, I know," said Cosmo. "Remember when I was lying there in the alley? Well, I could tell I was hurt pretty bad because it started to feel so nice to just lie there. I forced myself to get up, though. The surprise was when I looked back and saw my body still lying there. Right then I knew I had died."

"You're kidding," said Sammy.

Cosmo shook his head. "I'm telling you how it was."

Sammy sat up and crossed his arms. "So where've you been? Why didn't you show up before?"

"I've been busy, which is more than I can say for you, moping around like it's a paying job.

"What am I supposed to do?"

"Anything you want," said Cosmo. "Start eating, drinking and talking to people for starters."

Sammy slumped back into the net. "What's the use?" he mumbled, more to himself than to Cosmo. He lay there, staring at the empty frame on the opposite wall.

After a moment Cosmo said, "It's been pretty bad, huh?"

"The worst," said Sammy. Then he looked back at his brother and yelled. "Why'd you have to go and die? And why'd it have to be my fault?"

"Who said it was your fault?"

"Everybody does," said Sammy. "It was my idea to climb across that ladder, remember?"

"So? It was my idea to run to the rooftops in the first place," reminded Cosmo. "That's where we went wrong. We should have stood our ground."

"Yeah," said Sammy. "We should have pounded those guys, especially that redheaded jerk. I'll get even for you somehow, though. I promise."

"No, no, no. Don't waste your time."

"He's got it coming, Coz."

"It doesn't matter anymore."

Sammy looked down. "I guess nothing matters anymore."

"Knock it off. We got a lot to look forward to. At least I do. This ghost business is not as dull as you might think."

"Really," said Sammy, perking up at the prospects of having a ghost for a brother. "What do you do? What kind of powers do you have?"

"I don't know yet. I'm still learning the ropes."

"Can you scare people?"

"I scared you, didn't I."

"Can you read people's minds?"

"Easy as comic books."

"Hey, I know. Can you fly?"

"Uh, no. Not yet. I'm sort of grounded here for a while. You know, a person doesn't just die and automatically know all there is to know about being a ghost. It's gotta be learned, like anything else."

Sammy nodded as though this made all the sense in the world. Then he stopped. "You're not in school or nothing, are you?"

Cosmo laughed. "No," he said, "I just learn by listening."

"To who?"

"To the tide."

"Huh?"

"You heard me, the tide—twice a day as it rises and falls. You know that whispering sound the water makes against the piles? That's the tide talking to stranded spirits like myself. You'd be surprised at what you can learn if you know how to listen."

"Are there other spirits down here?"

"No, just me for the time being. Me and the seagull, that is. You know, the one those guys killed."

"What does the tide tell you?"

"Lots of things, but mainly that I got to get ready to leave here."

"What for?"

"Because ghosts belong somewhere else."

"Where?"

"I don't know yet; with each other, I suppose."

"We belong with each other, Coz."

"We did, Sammy. We sure did. But I've got to move on and you've got to help me."

"Me?"

"Yeah, you. You see, I've learned that the usual way for a ghost to leave the earth is to whisper a new idea into some kid's ear. It's sort of a farewell gift to the world that lifts him right out of here. But . . . "

"Wait a minute," said Sammy. "Do you mean every time a kid thinks up something new it's because a ghost has whispered in his ear?"

"That's right. And there's nothing strange about it. It's like when you read a book written by someone long dead. Same principle. The trouble is that a guy like me who dies without having learned anything worth passing on, well, he usually has to stay and fill out his destined lifespan."

"How long is that?"

"I don't know. Maybe a hundred years."

"That's great."

"Not for me, Sammy. Not now. I don't want to be an old wharf spook. There's so much more out there. I know there is. It would be like . . ." Cosmo looked around. " . . . like that candle passing up a chance to be a volcano."

Sammy glanced at the stubby lump of wax stuck in the wine bottle and tried to understand what his brother meant. Finally he sighed and said, "So what do you want me to do?"

"Nothing much," said Cosmo. "Just fix up our skiff and row me out in the bay on Halloween night."

"What for?"

"So I can rise with the tide," said Cosmo, his open hand rising with his words.

"I don't get it," said Sammy.

"It's simple," Cosmo explained. "Halloween is the spirits' holiday, when we can travel back and forth to whichever world we choose. Normally I wouldn't qualify, but this Halloween is special because there's going to be a full moon."

"So?"

"So it happens only once every nineteen years, and that's the most magical night there is. The moon's gravitational force will be a zillion times stronger than usual. Right at the stroke of midnight there'll be a great surge that can only be felt over the ocean's deepest waters. So if you can row me out over the trench at that time, I'll just dive in, recite a magic rhyme, and slide up a moon beam."

"That'd be something," said Sammy. "But why do you need me? Couldn't you just swim out there? You don't have to worry about drowning, do you?"

"'Course not, dumbbell. The thing is that without your help I'd never get ten feet out of the water. Your silly grief would weigh me down like an anchor."

"You mean you can feel it like that?"

"Even when you're sleeping," said Cosmo. Then he added, "So will you help?"

Sammy thought about it. "I guess so," he said. "But I'll need some help, too. I've never fixed up a skiff before or even rowed one."

"You gotta do it yourself, Sammy. You can't tell anyone. They'd think you were crazy."

"Jenko might not. He already said he'd help with the skiff. And he's got the strongest arms I've ever seen. He'll row us out there."

"It's up to you, Sammy. Just get me out there, okay?"

"Okay."

"So it's a deal. Let's shake on it," said Cosmo, holding out his hand. Sammy extended his arm expecting an airy shake, but Cosmo clasped it with a force that would have made a longshoreman wince. Sammy was about to holler when Cosmo released his grip and said, "All right then. We'll meet on Jenko's dock, say, ten-thirty on Halloween night. That's October thirty-first, just thirteen days away."

"Yeah," said Sammy, drawing in his sore hand, "but won't you come back before then?"

"Maybe, but I still have a lot of work to do," said Cosmo, "and I've got to keep listening for the rhyme."

Cosmo stood up and Sammy noticed his bare feet again. "What happened to your shoes?" he asked.

"Oh, yeah. How do you like my tux? Snazzy, huh? I figured you'd like to see it since you weren't at the funeral. I got a lot of compliments on it that day. But those cheapskates at the mortuary never gave me any shoes. I don't mind, though, It's not as if I have to worry about stepping in bird-doo."

Sammy smiled.

"So, see ya," Cosmo said, walking through the door like smoke through a screen.

Sammy's smile stretched into a huge yawn. He blew out the candle, lay down, and covered himself with a large piece of net that smelled like the sea. He was sound asleep in seconds.

CHAPTER SIX
Gao's Curse

SAMMY AWOKE EARLY the next morning, just as Monterey Bay and the entire West Coast began its magnificent, imperceptible roll toward sunlight. The shed was still cast in darkness, however, and for a panicky moment after his eyes shot open Sammy had no idea where he was. Then he recognized his surroundings and recalled with excitement—and a twinge of doubt—his visit from Cosmo.

Had he really come back as a ghost? Did he really need the skiff? Sammy banished his uncertainty. There was too much to do to lie there questioning himself. He rolled off the net and headed out the door.

Sammy swung across the pipe, scurried along the brace boards, and scrambled around piling after piling until he neared the wharf's edge. Under Jenko's studio he noticed something he had never seen before. Sitting on a girder, in a cubbyhole between two deck joists, was a pigeon's nest with two white eggs in it. The scraggly pad of twigs and straw seemed to be abandoned, but even so Sammy didn't dare touch it for fear his scent might rub off and the mother would certainly reject the eggs.

He moved on and soon came out under the wheeled ramp that led down to Jenko's floating dock. He saw his little rowboat lying hull up, just where he and Cosmo had left it. A few tethered skiffs floated lazily in the calm water, but most of those that Jenko let dock there were gone, having been rowed out to the lampara boats now working the bay.

Sammy glanced around and, seeing no one, climbed onto the ramp and hurried down to assess the work ahead. He circled the skiff twice, each time running his hand over the splintered gashes and pressing to find where the wood was damp and spongy. "How'm I ever going to fix this?" he moaned, and looked up longingly to the window of Jenko's studio.

The building loomed above the dock on stilt-like pilings. No one was there, but leaning on the railing across the way was old Gao. He stared sullenly at Sammy from beneath his huge straw cowboy hat. The fish peddler did not turn away or even nod when their eyes met. He just smoked his cigarette, stroked his wispy white mustache, and stared.

Sammy turned his attention back to the skiff, trying to figure out how he might make it watertight and what tools he might need. But he soon heard footsteps on the ramp and looked up to see old Gao shuffling down, the empty baskets on his shoulder pole swaying with each step.

Gao stopped at the skiff, opposite Sammy. The two stared warily at each other. Sammy studied the deep, intricate wrinkles on the old man's face. It was lined and crinkled like a century-old depth chart of Monterey Bay. Yet from behind his sagging lids, Gao stared with cold, ageless eyes.

Sammy felt strangely threatened, even though he had seen the harmless old man practically every day on the wharf. Then Sammy realized he had never spoken to him, that almost nobody did. Old Gao just stood there smoking and staring, smoking and staring.

"What do you want?" said Sammy.

Gao took another drag from the cigarette and threw it over

the edge. It landed in the water with an evil "Psst!" Then he said, "I want to know if your family going to sue me."

"Huh?" replied Sammy, completely confounded.

"I want to know if they going to start lawsuit against me and my building." Gao spoke with a brusk, raspy voice weighted by a heavy accent.

"I don't know what you're talking about. What building?"

"The one your brother fell off. Old Wharfside Fish Company. It belong to me. But your father and mother better not sue. I got it posted. Say 'Keep Out' everywhere."

"My father and mother are dead," said Sammy.

"Oh," said Gao. "Who that lady in the ambulance?"

"My aunt."

"She going to sue?"

Sammy was about to shake his head no, but the anger he felt that night on the wharf returned and he blurted out, "Why haven't you torn that thing down?"

Gao straightened up. "Too much money," he said.

"You should have," Sammy told him sadly. "You should have razed it to pieces."

"I didn't want to sell and give 'em satisfaction, either," added Gao.

"Give who satisfaction?"

"People who burn it out, that who! Those big shots on Cannery Row. They try to drive me out after I go into sardine business with my cousin."

"Why?"

"They greedy. Squid we do for years, catch by moonlight. Nobody care, except complain about smell when we dry 'em. But sardine big money, see. That different. We discover how to make fertilizer from offal—you know, waste product like head and tail. We biggest operation on the wharf and they burn us out. My cousin leave town after that. Practically all Chinese gone now, and we first ones develop fishing here."

"Not before the Italians," corrected Sammy.

Old Gao put down his shoulder pole and sat on the edge of the ramp. He took out a tobacco pouch from his coat pocket and began rolling another cigarette. "I tell you something," he said, "you all wrong. Chinese here even before most Italian set foot in America. Most Chinese come build railroad and end up stay for fishing. About four hundred settle over there on China Point back in 1850s."

"Is that why it's called China Point?"

"Yeah, but white people give it that name later, not Chinese. White people name everything." Gao licked the length of his cigarette, put it in his mouth, and dug around in his pockets for a match.

Sammy sat down on the skiff. "How come there's no Chinese there now?" he asked.

"They burn them out, too," said Gao, striking his match and lighting the cigarette. "They burn whole Chinatown back in 1906. Nothing proven, but eve'ybody know railroad send people down there. They been trying evict us for years."

"Were you there?"

"Yeah. I was down at my grandmother's house. Saw the whole thing. Looked out and saw puff of smoke, you know. The fire start inside the barn. Being north part of Chinatown, the wind blow that way, north to south, so naturally just burn like matchstick. Some people get hurt bad. At night down there I can still hear their scream."

"Couldn't anyone put it out?"

"Those people from railroad, they have shotgun and eve'ything, keeping people out. Don't even let them use the fire hose, that I remember. Chinese have one small water pump, you know, where the people draw their water. Somebody try to put a fire hose there but they wouldn't let him connect it. In a few hours, maybe couple hours, all burn down to the beach. Most Chinese just move away." Gao took another puff on his cigarette.

"How come they didn't rebuild?" asked Sammy.

The old man seemed to choke at the question. He coughed and coughed until at last he barked, "How they don't rebuild! How can they rebuild? They want the land back. You can't build without land. If they want them build again, they wouldn't burn them out. You know, they can kill Chinamen without they going to trial in those days." And then Gao chuckled.

Sammy thought it odd that he should laugh at such a thing. "I didn't know that," he said.

"There's a lot you don't know," replied Gao. "And people who do know want to forget. That's why they don't like see me around. I remind them of bad things. But that's history! They can't change it."

Sammy looked down and started picking at the paint flakes on the skiff. Gao, as if regretting the harshness of his words, asked in a kinder tone, "That your boat?"

Sammy nodded and kept picking.

"What you going to do with it?"

Sammy thought about his plans with Cosmo and realized that his brother was right: nobody would believe it. "I'm going to fix her up to go fishing," he said, "lay nets out by the breakwater."

"You think you big enough?"

Sammy didn't answer.

Gao began stroking his mustache. "What you going to do with the fish?"

"I don't know. Eat some, sell some."

"Why you don't sell to me?" proposed Gao. "I give good

price." Sammy looked up. "Nobody else want to deal with smallfry, you know. More trouble than it worth. But I buy sand dabs, rock cod, like that."

"All right," said Sammy.

Gao drew on his cigarette again and eyed the skiff closely. "That big job, though. How you going to fix it?"

"My friend Jenko is going to help."

"Jenko? The blind man?"

"Yeah," said Sammy defensively.

"I never meet him before, but I know who you mean. I like his new statue. It's a good joke."

"It wasn't any joke. It was the best statue of Columbus anyone ever made."

"Ah, Columbus big phony."

"Yeah, he only discovered America," Sammy replied sarcastically.

"No. Chinese here first, maybe one thousand year before Columbus. Some people think it just legend, but it all recorded. Five monk come during Liang Dynasty. Head monk named Huishen."

"Oh, yeah," challenged Sammy. "How'd they get here?"

"By boat, how you think?"

"I suppose you were here then, too?"

"No, but scientist finding proof all the time, big round stone anchors in the shallow water down south. They have hole in middle like donut. Those Chinese anchor. Ancient kind. So Columbus no big deal."

"You're just saying that because you're Chinese. You'd probably even say they were here before the Indians."

"Maybe so. Only speculation, but I read that during Ice Age some band of hunter from north China stalk mammoth and bison across the Bering Strait. Those first Indians; that why they look like Chinese."

"You're making this up."

"You don't have to believe me. I don't care. But you too young to think you got nothing to learn." Old Gao grabbed his shoulder pole and stood up. "I got to go meet the boats. You going to start work, too?"

"Yeah."

"Good." Gao started off and then halted. "You know, that work going to cost money. How you going to pay for material?"

"I don't know."

The old peddler reached into his pocket and pulled out a thick roll of bills. He peeled off a ten dollar note and handed it to Sammy. "Here, I give you advance on the fish you sell me, okay?"

"Sure," said Sammy, holding the bill in both hands.

"But you got to promise you won't sue," said Gao.

"I was never going to," said Sammy. As Gao turned to leave, Sammy added, "You should promise something too—to tear your building down. It's not good for anything anymore."

"Maybe you're right," said Gao. "I could sell now those other companies out of business. I already showed 'em good."

"You did?"

Gao looked left and right, then leaned closer and whispered, "I put curse on the bay, made all sardine disappear."

Sammy watched in awe as old Gao shuffled back up the ramp, his baskets swinging as before.

Shortly after Gao left, Sammy realized he couldn't put it off any longer. He slid off the skiff, swatted the seat of his pants clean, and set off to face Aunt Nastina. There wasn't another soul in sight as he headed up the wharf. None of the businesses were open yet, not even the breakfast joints.

Sammy was halfway home when a garbage truck swung into view. It dropped into low gear with a rev and a grind, and a brawny battalion of garbage men, each shouldering huge metal barrels, leaped off the running boards. They bounded in all directions like spilled wheel-bearings and virtually attacked the garbage cans on both sides of the wharf. They wrestled them up, banged them empty, and threw them back down, never tarrying to pick up what was spilled.

The stink and racket soon surrounded Sammy, and if he hadn't jumped out of the workers' way they might have scooped him up too, with all the other rubbish and rat food.

The Lighthouse Gift Shop was dark when Sammy slunk past it. The sign on the door said CLOSED, and the jewelry cases in the window were empty. Sammy slid around the corner. From the rear landing he could see that all the lights were off upstairs as well. She must still be asleep, he thought.

Sammy crept quietly up the back stairs, wisely skipping the creakiest steps. But the whole staircase complained under his weight as if in a conspiracy to betray his presence. He turned the knob and found it unlocked. Had she been expecting him, he wondered.

Sammy slowly pushed open the door and this time the hinges announced his arrival with a long jagged whine. He peered into the dimness until his eyes made out the spiral staircase. He then stole into the flat, leaving the door ajar so that it wouldn't squeak again. He tiptoed past his aunt's bedroom to the stairs, and as he laid his hand on the cold rail he heard a shriek that would have made him jump out of his socks if he had been wearing any.

"Sammy! Is that you?"

Before he could answer, Aunt Nastina appeared at her door like a ghoulish apparition. She had on a long dark robe and her face was caked with a white cream that made her eyes look like sockets in a skull. Her hair was bound under a black hairnet.

"Where have you been?" she shrieked again.

"N-n-nowhere," he stammered.

"Nowhere! You've been gone two nights. Where were you?"

He confessed reluctantly, "Just under the wharf."

Aunt Nastina swooped over and grabbed him by the arm. "Do-you-know-how-much-trouble-you've-caused?" she said as she jerked him back and forth. Her fingernails dug into his skin and Sammy cowered against the bottom step.

"I'm sorry, I'm sorry," he pleaded.

"Sorry! The whole wharf's been looking for you." She released her grip and slapped him hard across the face. "Even the police!"

Sammy's left ear went numb and he covered his head with both arms. Aunt Nastina began to cry. She knelt down and hugged her nephew close. "Don't you know what a scare you gave us?" she sobbed. "We thought you had jumped off the wharf and drowned."

Sammy heard her with his good ear and felt truly sorry now. "I know how to swim," he comforted.

She squeezed him tighter against her and rocked gently. From outside came the din of the garbage truck heading off the wharf. Aunt Nastina sighed. "This is one Wednesday I'm glad those men woke me up," she said, "or I might never have heard you." Then she held him at arm's length. "Look at you. You look like a garbage man yourself. Your hair's a mess, your clothes are filthy. And what are those, your good pajamas?"

Sammy looked down at the soiled and ragged cuffs coming out of his pant legs.

"Come on," she said, plucking him up and marching him down the hall. "You need a bath." Once in the bathroom, she put the stopper in the tub, turned on the hot water, and poured in some soap powder. Steam rose in the room and clouded up the mirror. "Get in there and wash up," she ordered, and left him to undress.

Sammy was soaping up happily when Aunt Nastina returned with a towel and some fresh clothes. She set them on the floor and sat down on the toilet seat cover. She had wiped off her face cream.

"How could you have been under the wharf all that time?" she asked. "Babe and Benny looked there."

"I was in my shed."

"What shed?"

"Mine and Cosmo's. We built it a long time ago."

"Haven't I always told you not to go down there?" Sammy scrubbed his face with the wash rag rather than answer. "Since you don't know how to mind, I'm going to see that Ratzo's boys tear that shed apart, board by board."

Sammy was tempted to say, "They'll never find it." But he didn't.

"And until then," continued Aunt Nastina, "I'm not letting you out of my sight. So hurry up and wash your hair. You're going to work with me."

"I can't, Auntie. I got other work to do."

"What other work?"

"I have to fix up that skiff, the one Cosmo and I told you about."

"Are you still fooling around with that thing?"

"I have to. Cosmo needs ... " Sammy stopped himself. "Cosmo needs to know I didn't just forget about it."

"Well, I think you ought to. I need you to help me. I'm starting inventory today."

Sammy tried hard to think of another excuse. Finally, he said, "Okay, but old Gao's gonna be mad."

"Old Gao? What does he have to do with this?"

"He wants to buy my fish . . . " Sammy stopped himself again, but it was too late.

"Your fish! What fish? Didn't I say you were never to take that boat on the water?"

"No, I didn't say fish," lied Sammy. "I said skiff. He wants to buy my skiff. He's already given me ten dollars to start work on it." Sammy swallowed deep. He never realized how hard it was not to tell the truth. But he just couldn't tell everything, not yet at least.

"Ten dollars? You have ten dollars?"

"In my pants there." Sammy pointed with a soapy hand.

Aunt Nastina leaned over and searched through Sammy's pockets until she found the bill. "I'll just hang on to this until I have a chance to straighten out that crazy Chinaman."

"He's not crazy," said Sammy. "Did you know that he used to own the biggest fish company on the wharf until someone burnt him out?"

"Yes, yes, but that's all history now," she said as she stood up. "Hurry out of there. I've got a shop to open."

CHAPTER SEVEN
Spook On The Loose

THE CALENDAR on the wall above the desk said Sunday, October 23. Four whole days had passed and Sammy had spent every one of them locked in Aunt Nastina's dungeon of a storeroom.

It was a narrow, windowless room down three steps at the rear of the shop. Dusty vases, candlesticks and other merchandise crowded the shelves. Cardboard boxes were stacked from floor to ceiling against the back wall, and even in front of the rear door, like a barricade against burglars.

True to her word, Aunt Nastina hadn't let Sammy out of her sight, except in the storeroom. She brought him there every morning and had him take inventory while she worked out front. He counted stock all day, stopping only when she did, for lunch. In the evenings he'd go home so number-weary that after dinner he'd just fall into bed, where he continued to tally things in his dreams.

Sammy was sitting now in a pile of packing paper on the floor by the desk, counting the tiger shells in one of the last three open cases. But at number thirty-one his eyes were drawn again to the Hooper's Dry Dock calendar. "Halloween is a week away," it seemed to shout, "and you haven't done a thing about the skiff!"

But what could he do? Both doors were locked. And even if

he could sneak out, he wouldn't have time to do a lick of work before Aunt Nastina caught up with him. Besides, she said she wouldn't stand for any more of his "childish escapades."

Ah, maybe it doesn't matter anyway, he thought. Maybe he never really saw Cosmo's ghost. Or if he had, it was just a vision brought on by too many hours alone and without eating.

Sammy finished with the shells and wrote "Tigers-49" in a big yellow tablet on the chair. He began counting the souvenir spoons in the next box, but his mind wandered again and he soon lost track. "Shoot!" he said, and started over, this time counting out loud, "One, two, three, four . . . "

Then, as if conjured up by the challenge of Sammy's doubts, Cosmo's astral vapor seeped in through the air vent beneath the steps. Sammy watched slack-jawed as his brother took shape, tuxedo and all.

"Boo," said Cosmo.

"Boo yourself," said Sammy, smiling.

"Having fun?"

"No. I've been stuck here for days. I didn't think you'd ever come back."

"I didn't think you'd ever come back," mimicked Cosmo in a crybaby voice. "What the heck's the matter with you? You're supposed to be getting the skiff ready for me."

"I couldn't! I've had to finish this."

"So finish! Put down ten, twenty, a hundred! What do you care how much stuff she's got here?" Cosmo stood menacingly over his brother.

"It's my job," said Sammy.

"You mean you'd rather count spoons than help me?"

"No! Auntie's making me. I didn't want to."

"Well, tell her then! Tell her there's such a thing as child labor laws. Tell her it's a sin to work on Sunday. Tell her anything!"

"You tell her," said Sammy, feeling bullied.

"Maybe I will." Cosmo kicked Sammy's box with his bare foot and the spoons went skidding all over the floor.

"What'd you do that for?"

"Face it, you don't want me to leave. You want me to stay and be a dumb wharf spook. All right then, I'll act like one—making messes, playing tricks, scaring people. How else do you expect a ghost to amuse himself for a hundred years?"

Sammy sighed. "Relax," he said. "I'll row you out. Just wait and see."

Cosmo sat on the steps and sulked. He was the glummest looking ghost Sammy had ever seen.

They suddenly heard keys jangling at the door. It swung open and there stood Aunt Nastina.

"Who are you talking to?" she asked.

Sammy looked at Cosmo. "No one," he said. "It's just me here, counting. I was counting."

"Aren't you finished yet?"

"Tell her you're going on strike," suggested Cosmo.

"Shut up!" whispered Sammy.

"What did you say to me?" asked Aunt Nastina.

"Nothing," said Sammy. "Really. It wasn't me. I mean it wasn't anything."

"Let me see the pad," said Aunt Nastina, starting down the steps. Sammy held his breath as she came to Cosmo, but she walked right through him as if he weren't there. "You sure made a mess down here," she said.

Sammy jumped up and put the tablet on the desk for her.

"Fine, fine," she said after skimming through it, "but your penmanship has gotten sloppier every day. Maybe it's time you went back to school." Sammy sagged at the very mention of the subject. "I probably could have even taken you to church today. You do seem to have gotten over your foolishness. Nothing like a little hard work to do the trick."

"Tell her you know just the kind of work to do next," said Cosmo.

"Shhh!" said Sammy.

"What?" asked Aunt Nastina.

"S-sure, whatever you think," said Sammy.

Aunt Nastina shot him a cross look. "Listen," she said. "I'm going up to start lunch, but there's something I want you to do before eating. I want you to go apologize to Sergeant Abner for all the trouble you caused. Can I trust you to do that?"

"Do I have to?"

"Yes. It's only right. And then you're to come straight home. Is that clear?"

"I guess so."

"Get going then."

As soon as Aunt Nastina was up the steps, Sammy whispered to Cosmo, "You want to come?"

"Might as well," said Cosmo.

It was gray and drizzly out, but pearly bright to Sammy, who felt like a prisoner on reprieve and in cahoots again with his old partner-in-crime. He swaggered up the wharf, shoulder-to-shoulder with Cosmo, who was invisible to all the world save Sammy. Only the gulls and pigeons lining the rooftops sensed his ghostly presence. But they kept quiet about it, letting the music of Benny's organ carry the moment.

The boys found Sergeant Abner's booth dark and its doors closed.

"He must be off today," said Cosmo. "Let's go start on the skiff."

"No," said Sammy. "He's here. His barrel is out."

"Aw, come on. It's our only chance."

"I don't think we should, Coz. Don't you see, this is Aunt Nastina's test. If I take off she'll never let me out again."

"Forget it then, ya big sissy."

"Just wait here," said Sammy. He walked over and crouched among the few tourists standing around Buffa's rug. The monkey spotted him at once and climbed chattering into his arms.

"Well, looka who's back," said Benny, still cranking music out of his three-legged organ. "Easy, Buffa. Easy." Benny flicked the leash and then pulled her toward others in the group. "She 'appy to see you. You know, we both ran aroun' crazy for you de udda day."

"I know," said Sammy, standing up.

"Buffa, she hadda ball down dere. But me, I t'ought I was gonna end up a sea line dinner. No more, huh? You wanna crawl aroun unna da wharf, fine. But not me."

Sammy nodded.

"So *che fai?* Whatcha doing now?"

"Looking for Sergeant Abner."

"Ha! You betta look in one a da nice warm *ristorante.*" Buffa then began cheeping wildly and Benny shook the leash again. "Buffa, *zita!* Be quiet!"

Sammy looked over and saw Cosmo standing on Buffa's tail and unbuckling her collar. "What are you doing?" he cried, half under his breath. He ran to Buffa and tried to grab the frightened monkey, but her collar and leash now fell to the ground and she scampered up the wharf's railing.

"Why you do dat for?" yelled Benny. He rushed toward Buffa, but tripped over his organ, which fell with a resounding crash of expiring notes. Buffa leaped into the air and went scurrying down the wharf, with Benny chasing after her, crying, '*Vene ca! Vene ca!* Come back! Come back!"

Cosmo just stood there with a silly smirk on his face.

"What's the big idea?" said Sammy.

"Nothing. I just thought she might be tired of that stupid leash."

"You're what's stupid. Come on."

Still thinking it wise to obey his aunt, Sammy hustled down the wharf. He peeked in the windows of all the cafes and restaurants, ignoring diners' dirty looks. He did observe that most of the businesses had their Halloween decorations up. Paper witches, skeletons, and arched-back cats were taped on many of the windows.

Angelo's had the best decorations of all. Stapled to its menu board was an orange and black poster advertising a costume party. And the entrance was guarded by two jagged-tooth Jack-o'-lanterns. Sammy looked between the carved pumpkins and through the glass door, and spotted Sergeant Abner eating at the bar. He then read the sign on the door. NO ONE UNDER 21 ALLOWED, it said.

"Gonna buy me a whisky?" asked Cosmo.

"Be quiet for once," said Sammy as he pushed open the heavy door and walked in.

A fire was burning in the hooded brick fireplace in the center of the room. Babe and a few other fishermen were leaning back in their chairs, talking quietly, sipping their drinks, and warming their feet. Angelo and his brothers—the cook and bartender—were playing cutthroat pinochle in the corner near the old upright piano. And Sergeant Abner was bent hungrily over a bowl of clam chowder.

None of them noticed as the under-aged interloper circled the fireplace. Sammy passed the row of burlap-covered barrels that served as barstools. He stood for a second eye-level with Sergeant Abner's holstered pistol, and then tapped him on the knee. The off-duty officer looked down in mid-slurp. He gulped, wiped his chin, and said, "Well, if it ain't Monterey's most-wanted man."

The fishermen and cardplayers looked up, expecting to see a notorious fugitive. But on spotting Sammy, they realized Abner's greeting was a joke and there would be no excitement to break up a lazy Sunday afternoon. Disappointed, they returned to the business of idling.

Sammy hung his head in embarrassment and mumbled something.

"What?" asked Abner.

"I said I'm sorry," repeated Sammy. "I didn't mean for everyone to have to look for me."

"Oh, didn't you? Well, I got news for you. A kid with as many friends as you can't expect to disappear without anyone taking notice."

Sammy didn't say anything.

"But what still bugs me is that we couldn't find you. Agnestina said you were in some shed under the wharf. Is that right?"

"Yeah."

"What were you doing there?"

"Just . . . thinking."

"Yep, that'll get you into trouble every time." Sergeant Abner laughed. "But you're back for good, right? No more monkey business?"

"No," said Sammy, looking around for Cosmo.

The mighty opening of Beethoven's Fifth Symphony suddenly burst from the piano in the corner: DAT DAT DAT DAA! DAT DAT DAT DAA! Coming from a playerless instrument, the eight-note motto sounded more like fate knocking at the door than the composer had ever imagined.

Cards and money flew into the air, and Babe was so startled he fell over backwards in his chair, spilling his drink all over himself.

Only Sammy could see his tuxedoed brother attacking the keyboard like a virtuoso in debut. "Not again!" he wailed, and ran over to try to shut the lid over the keys. But Cosmo held it open with his head and kept playing.

"What's going on here?" shouted Angelo.

"You ought to have that thing looked at," said Babe, trembling.

"I've never seen anything like it!" marveled Sergeant Abner. "Sammy, get away from there. It might explode or something."

There was a sudden scrape of chairs as the pinochle players got up and moved back to the bar. Angelo pulled Sammy with him.

"Do you really think it could explode?" asked Babe.

"I don't know," said Abner. "Some joker must have rigged it up somehow."

"What were you doing over there?" Angelo asked Sammy. "What are you doing in here at all?"

"Nothing!" said Sammy, his voice shrill and defensive. "I didn't have anything to do with it."

The music stopped now as abruptly as it had started. Cosmo stood up and bowed to his audience. "What'd you think of that little ditty?" he asked Sammy. "Some show of spookmanship, huh? Livened up this place pretty good."

Sammy shook his head in disgust. Everyone else just stared at the silent piano. Then they turned to each other as if to ask, "Did we hear what we thought we heard?" No one ventured an answer. But Sergeant Abner dutifully got up to look behind the upright for wires.

Angelo went the opposite direction — behind the bar — and poured himself a shot of brandy. He offered one to Babe, who, after getting up off the floor, waved it away. "No more for me," he said. "I'm not gonna touch another drop long as I live."

The other fishermen must have felt the same way, for they bolted toward the door. After all of them had funneled out, Benny, looking half-trampled and completely dispirited, stood facing in. All the color had left his once-cheerful face and even his mustache drooped. He was holding his shattered organ and Buffa's empty leash.

"Didn't you catch her?" asked Sammy.

The veins in Benny's neck bulged. "You!" he spat. "Is alla you fault! You ruin me!" He held up the organ and leash for all to see. "My monkey's gone. My music is broke. 'E's ruin me. I'm finish."

Benny dropped the leash and organ and staggered toward Sammy with arms held out as if to throttle him. But Angelo's brothers grabbed him first and sat him down on a barstool, where he began to cry. Angelo handed him the shot of brandy he had poured for Babe. As he drank it, everyone looked accusingly at Sammy.

"I didn't do anything!" he said. "Honest!" Sammy looked to Cosmo for help and saw him crawling under the cardtable picking up the fallen money. Sammy ran over to him. "Get out of here!" he said. "You're ruining everything."

"Here, take this," said Cosmo, handing him a fistful of dollars.

"I don't want it."

"Get away from there!" yelled Angelo from behind the bar. "What are you doing with that money?"

Sammy threw it down just as Sergeant Abner grabbed him by the collar. "Let go," he said. "I'm taking you home."

Sammy twisted around to plead with the sergeant, but saw Cosmo lifting the gun from his holster. "Not that!" he screamed,

and tried to push it back in. Abner grabbed for the gun too
and—BANG!—a shot rang out. The bullet zinged across the
room, richocheted off the fireplace hood, and shattered the
bottle of brandy on the bar. Angelo, just inches away, slumped
to the floor in a cold faint.

"That does it," said Abner. I'm taking you to the station.

Meanwhile, back at Aunt Nastina's flat, no foot ever tapped
so furiously. Nastina had been sitting at the kitchen table for
twenty minutes now, wait-wait-waiting for Sammy to get
back and tap-tap-tapping out her anger and frustration.

At first she tried to find excuses for Sammy's tardiness, and
imagined Sergeant Abner keeping him over with a stern
lecture. But she had already heated up last night's minestrone,
cut a salad, and set the table. And after pouring Sammy's
milk, she realized Abner would never expend the energy for
such a marathon scolding. So she sat down and began to
silently rehearse one of her own: ("Didn't I say to come
straight home? Is this the way you mind? Is this the thanks I
get? . . . ") But the more she went over it the madder she got,
until the tapping of her foot began to sound like the ticking of
a time-bomb. And all that pent-up anger slowly burned in her
stomach.

The soup, by contrast, had fast cooled. Steam no longer
rose from the bowl. Aunt Nastina noticed this and held her
palm over it. "Cold as bilge water," she declared. Then she
exploded: "Damn it! Where is that kid?"

She was answered by a knock at the door. "And now I have
to treat you like company?" she called out. The door swung
open and Sammy stumbled in. Behind him came Sergeant
Abner, Benny, and Angelo—as grim faced as a school of
gopher cod.

"Oh, my God! What now?" she cried.

"There's been some trouble," said Abner. "I just dropped by to tell you I'm taking him to the station."

Aunt Nastina stood up. "What for? What's happened?"

"Disturbing the peace. Malicious mischief. Resisting arrest. You name it. The kid's been on a rampage. I'm taking him in."

"Don't put me in jail," begged Sammy. "I don't want to be locked up anymore."

"Sorry, kiddo. You've got some explaining to do and I can't think of a better place to do it."

"But I didn't do anything."

"*Basta!*" barked Benny. "Enough widda lies or you make t'ings worse."

"I want to know what's been going on," demanded Aunt Nastina. "I sent him out to apologize to you."

"Apologize, sure," said Abner, "but then all hell broke loose. The piano in Angelo's bar went berserk. Sammy started running around like a loony himself. And the next thing I knew he was going for my gun."

"I coulda been killed by that shot!" piped in Angelo. "I'm pressing charges."

"An' don' forget my Buffa," said Benny. "'E let my Buffa go for no reason."

"I didn't!" repeated Sammy.

"Den who did?" asked Benny.

Sammy took a deep breath. "I can't tell you."

"Let's go," said Abner. "Nastina, you're going to have to come down later too."

"Take him," she said. "Lock him up and throw away the key. I've had it. Just when I think he's straightened out, he pulls something like this. I can't take anymore. I've done all I know how to do." She collapsed crying in her chair and grabbed for a napkin to wipe away the tears.

"Are you happy now?" Abner asked Sammy. "Are you satisfied? Look at what you're doing to your aunt. You ought to be ashamed of yourself."

"I'm not!" yelled Sammy. "And I'm not going to jail. There's no time."

"No time for what?" said Abner.

"I can't say."

"Why not?"

"I promised."

"Promised who? What's going on here?"

Sammy turned away, toward Benny and Angelo. They looked at him with serious, pleading eyes.

"Don't be afraid to speak up," said the restaurant owner. "Take it from me, some promises got no business being kept."

Benny nodded in agreement. "We suppossa be friends, no? You can tella who."

Sammy wanted to tell them the truth. He wanted to trust them. He had to! And before he knew it, the words slipped out of his mouth: "It's Cosmo."

The silence thickened.

"It's the truth," he said. "I've seen him as plain as I see you now. He's still here, learning how to be a ghost. He's causing all the trouble because he's afraid I won't let him leave. That's why I have to fix up the skiff. It's the only way. And we've only got until Halloween. I just can't go to jail."

Everyone stared at Sammy as if he were some unknown species that had crawled up from the ocean floor. Then Benny spoke: "Losing you brother musta be awful, but it be joost as bad for me to lose Buffa. You shouldna let 'er go."

"I didn't do it, I tell you! But don't worry, Cosmo told me he'd find her and bring her back to you. He never meant any harm, really."

"Oh, yeah?" said Sergeant Abner. "And what about shooting a firearm in a crowded bar? That's not what I'd call harmless."

"Coz said it was your fault; you pulled the trigger. He was only going to hide the gun for a while. Just for a joke, you know, like playing the piano."

"That was him?" asked Angelo.

Sammy nodded.

"Aaaiiieee!" screamed Aunt Nastina. "I can't listen to any more of this nonsense."

Abner walked over and patted her shoulder. "Sammy, go to your room for now," he instructed. "We've got a few things to talk about here."

Sammy did as he was told, but only shut the door part way so he could hear his fate being decided.

"The kid needs help, Nastina," Abner began. "I was going to give him a good scare down at the station, but I think he's way past the point where it would do any good. He really believes that story."

"Impossible," she sniffed. "It's just something he made up to get out of trouble."

"I don't think so. I've never heard anyone lie that good. My guess is it's psychological, something he's imagined to deal with Cosmo's passing."

"A lie is a lie," said Nastina. "I've pampered his grief long enough. He has to learn to get over things like the rest of us."

"Ghosts, hah!" bellowed Angelo. "The poor kid's lost his marbles."

Benny was deep in thought, curling the end of his mustache. "What do you think?" Abner asked him.

"I t'ink is no good fool aroun' widda ghos'."

"You don't mean you believe him?" said Angelo.

"I don' know. But in de Old Country we don' take no chance widda spirits. I remember one lady in my village, she had *'il mal occhio'* — da Evil Eye. One look make wine go sour."

"Ah, that's nothing but peasant ignorance."

"No, no. Da ghos' a dead cats usta follow her aroun'. All da animal go wild when she passa by, like Buffa did, even before Sammy gotta close. Hmmm . . . I don' know. Just t'inking about it scare me." Benny made a quick sign of the cross.

"Well, it would explain that piano music," admitted Angelo. "But we don't believe in superstitiousness here in America."

"I still say it's mental," contended Abner.

"But what can I do with him?" said Aunt Nastina. "I've got to go back to work and I can't even trust him alone in his own room anymore."

"A couple of nights in jail will knock it out of him," said Angelo. "I'm still planning on pressing charges."

Sergeant Abner frowned. "Cut it out with the charges, Ange. You'd only be pressing your luck."

"Well, you can't have him walking around loose!" he replied.

"Why not?" said Abner. "I say we humor him. Let him fix up that boat if he likes. Tell him he can even row it out for Halloween. It might be all he needs to get the whole thing out of his system."

"Oh, all right," said Nastina, "if you really think it'll help."

"I don' know," cautioned Benny. "Some spirits you can't joost yumor."

CHAPTER EIGHT
A Death Defied

THE ONCE STORM-BATTERED SKIFF now rested high and dry atop two sawhorses on Jenko's dock. Scattered around it were tools, scraps of sandpaper, a half-eaten meatball sandwich, and a green, size-eight sweatshirt rolled inside-out.

A steady scratching came from inside the boat, where Sammy was hunched on his knees, tirelessly sanding the sideboards. Though it was chilly out, he wore only a sleeveless white undershirt, which was flecked with paint flakes. He had started in with a scraper at daybreak, and had already taken several layers of color off the outside. The wood's dark grain showed through in places and a fresh sawdusty smell was in the air.

It was Saturday the twenty-ninth, but Sammy was no longer worried about missing his deadline. The little flat-bottomed boat had received more loving attention over the past week than at any time since it was built. In fact, if Whisky Breath, the original owner, had passed by, he would not have recognized it as the beached wreck he had given away.

The fisherman had mistakenly presumed the skiff's working days were over. He probably expected that nature would take its course and that the waves would pound it into so much driftwood, which the hobos who slept up near the railroad tracks would gather for their bonfires. This wouldn't have been such a terrible fate, as fates go. But the brothers had had other ideas, and now Sammy's efforts were giving the vessel a second life and a chance to fulfill a much greater destiny.

He began work on the boat Monday morning, after waking Jenko. The sculptor had been up late the night before, as usual, and was snoring away like a congested walrus when Sammy called on him. It took several good shakes to rouse him. And even then, he was so groggy he couldn't follow all Sammy's jabber about ghosts and skiffs and full moons and ten dollar bills. Jenko finally had to interrupt.

"Whoa, whoa!" he said. "If you need the boat to let your brother move on, then say no more, I'll help."

Jenko sent Sammy to the dock with an armload of tools. Ten minutes later he came tapping down the ramp himself, with the aid of his cane. Jenko inspected the craft thoroughly. His knowing hands pressed and carressed it as if it were one of his own works of art.

"Not bad, not bad," he would say as he felt the various joints and gouges. "Could be worse." But when he got to the rear of the boat, he said, "Uh-oh! This looks like trouble." He took out a penknife and began poking the stern board. "Yep, the transom is rotted. It's got to go. Maybe the corner post too."

Jenko then wrote out a shopping list to be filled at Hooper's. It included one pound of caulking cotton, a quart of seam pitch, a box of galvanized flathead screws, sandpaper, glue, putty, and four square-feet of half-inch marine-grade plywood. "Be sure it's marine grade," repeated Jenko.

Sammy took the list and ran home to get old Gao's money from Aunt Nastina. But she refused to hand it over. She said she was going to open a bank account for him instead, to which she would generously deposit an extra four dollars for the four days he had taken inventory.

Crestfallen, Sammy returned to Jenko's dock. "Don't sulk, man!" he chided. "You'll have to improvise, that's all."

Jenko went back to his studio and Sammy spent the rest of the day scavenging the wharf for substitute materials.

First stop was the secret shed. He climbed there with Jenko's claw hammer hooked in his belt loop. As soon as he lit a new candle, he took the hammer and broke up the clam box stools so he could reuse the nails. He tapped the bent ones straight and tossed them all into the match can, which he lugged back to the dock.

He returned to the shed twice more; once to gather all the rope he and Cosmo had collected over the years, and then again to tear down the plywood door. He didn't want to do it, but he didn't know where else to get the wood.

Yet that stubborn sheet of knot holes didn't want to come off its hinges and Sammy had to really wrestle with it. It got the best of him at first, leaving his hands riddled with slivers. And afterwards, when he did pull it free, he felt even worse: like he had beat up a friend.

Before leaving the shed, Sammy looked around at all his stuff—the broken propeller, the pile of net, the picture of his mother and father. He sensed he wouldn't be back for a very long time, so he untacked the photo and slipped it into his back pocket. Then he blew out the candle.

Sammy's treasure hunt also took him back to the rooftops. He had some trepidation about going up there, but remembered seeing all the junk strewn about and thought some of it might be of use. On approaching the art gallery, however, he noticed that the crates which had been stacked up to the balcony were gone.

"Ah, forget it," he moaned, half-relieved. But then he recalled Jenko's words: "Don't sulk, man. Improvise!"

So he did. Sammy walked confidently up the gallery stairs and pretended to admire the paintings on the walls. To his surprise, he became genuinely interested in the seascapes. He was fascinated by how certain artists captured the color and motion of waves, how each used different brush strokes and textures, and how the paintings changed when viewed from a distance.

The saleslady seemed to recognize Sammy as a serious browser and smiled approvingly. But the moment some adult customers entered, she turned her attention to them. Sammy took that opportunity to step out on the balcony and climb hugger-mugger onto the roof. He bent the rain gutter, but was happy to discover he could pull himself up without Cosmo's help.

Sammy surveyed the long row of pitched roofs shrouded with wires. The sight did not disturb him as before, though he still felt strangely out of place there.

The pickings were slimmer than he thought. The only items of possible use were a raggedy mop and a sticky black can of roofing tar. He gathered them up and tiptoed to the edge by the bar. Leaning over, he peered down into the alley he and Cosmo had leaped across. Then he dropped the stuff over the edge. He flinched when they banged against the planks below, for it reminded him of the awful crash of Cosmo's body.

Sammy glanced over at old Gao's packing house. He could almost see Cosmo and himself clinging to the overhang. He no longer blamed the burnt-out shell of a building, but the sight of it still filled him with sadness and regret. He couldn't help it; he longed for Coz to be alive again, and not just a show-offy spook who only cared about leaving. Sammy knew he should be fixing the skiff with him, not for him. And the thought made him mad. At first it was a vague, unsatisfying kind of anger, but it improved as he focused it on one person: the sadistic oaf with the red hair. Sammy felt such loathing for the boy that he was grinding his teeth without realizing it.

Eventually, Sammy eased himself down to the balcony. He waited there until the lady and her customers stood facing one of the large oil paintings, and then stepped back inside. "Thanks a lot," he said on his way down the stairs. "Oh, thank you," replied the lady. "Come again."

Once outside, Sammy retrieved his plunder and carried it back to Jenko's dock. He stored it there for the night, which seemed to fall hours earlier than normal.

The rest of the week zoomed by even faster. Sammy worked nonstop against the deadline, mostly on his own. Jenko showed up only to advise him on various stages of the job. On Tuesday, for example, Jenko brought down the sawhorses and a pocket full of screws and explained in great detail how to replace the transom. Then he left.

Sammy knocked out the old board all right—crowbarred it to smithereens. And measuring the new piece was easy; he just leaned the door against the stern and scribed it with a pencil. But he had a heck of a time cutting the wood and screwing it into place. The saw jammed and went Wwwonnnggg! on every down stroke. And the stupid screws wouldn't go all the way in.

Sammy finally gave up and used the clam box nails. But even that was difficult. The hammer was heavy and he needed two hands to swing it. And still he missed the nails as often as he hit them. He ended up bending quite a few, but he dabbed the heads with roofing tar so they wouldn't take in water. Jenko checked the work that evening, but he couldn't tell that nails had been used instead of screws.

On Wednesday, Sammy patched the two gouges in the sideboards. Following Jenko's instructions, he chipped away the splintered wood and squared out the holes. Then he took what remained of the shed door and cut pieces to back the holes and pieces to fit in them. Jenko showed up just when Sammy started to nail the patches to the boat.

"Wait a minute," he said. "What are you doing hammering? Nails will work loose. Don't you have any screws left?"

"Yeah, a few," said Sammy. "But they keep getting stuck."

"Well, why didn't you say so?" said Jenko. "I have a secret solution for just such sticky situations."

He hustled off to his studio and returned in a few minutes with a small bar of soap. He told Sammy to rub the screws against it before starting them. He tried it, and sure enough they slipped in like straws through a snow cone.

On Thursday, Jenko showed Sammy how to recaulk the skiff, an age-old technique that allows joints to shrink and swell without leaking. They first rolled the skiff over and Sammy unscrewed the keel and raked out the old caulking between and around the two plywood sheets of the hull. He used one of Jenko's dull chisels for the job and was careful not to open the seams too much. Then he cut the strings off the mop and layed them in, expertly twisting the cotton as he pressed it home with the chisel.

When Sammy ran out of cotton, Jenko had him finish with oakum, which was nothing more than strands picked from the old ropes he had brought from the shed. "It's what shipwrights used in Columbus' day," Jenko pointed out. By dusk, Sammy had sealed the seams with the last of the tar and refastened the keel.

On Friday, he reinforced the oar blocks and braced the rear and middle thwarts. Jenko said it was okay to use nails for these jobs, and Sammy did so. He hammered most of them

straight and true, sometimes using only one hand. However, just when he felt he had gotten the swing of it, and started thinking about what he might name the skiff, he bashed his left thumb with the hammer.

"Ai-yowww!" he hollered, rolling his head back and squeezing his eyelids shut. He sucked air through his teeth to keep from crying out again. But it hurt so much he could see the pain throbbing like rings of lightning against a black sky. All he could do was rock there on his knees inside the boat and cradle his poor thumb against his chest. That's how Jenko found him when he returned.

Sammy told him about the accident, expecting some sympathy. But his mentor congratulated him instead. "It's a rite of passage," he told Sammy, who had no idea what that meant. "Every boat builder since Noah has banged his thumb. You've joined the brotherhood."

"Big deal," said Sammy.

"It is," said Jenko. "Oh, it'll hurt for a few days, and the nail may turn black and fall off. But over time a new pink one will sprout out of the cuticle. You'll be witness to a miracle of nature."

Sammy was hardly comforted by the knowledge, but the pain subsided enough for him to finish hammering. Only then did he prepare to paint, a tedious job, particularly with a damaged digit, that took him into Saturday.

Throughout the busy week, many of the wharf locals dropped by to see how Sammy's work was going. Some, like Ratzo and Nastina, shook their heads at the folly of a ten year old repairing a boat. But most were impressed by his progress. Especially old Gao, who showed up first thing every morning. He seldom spoke, but always gave an approving nod.

Sergeant Abner also swung by regularly while on his rounds.

He'd lean over the railing and say, "Looks good from here."
Then he'd wink, touch his cap in salute, and be off.

Babe, on the other hand, would hang around for hours. He
was forever complimenting Sammy on his craftsmanship and
capacity for hard work. "You make me tired just watching,"
he said. He kept promising to lend a hand when he got some
free time, but in the end his only contributions were some
sandpaper and turpentine left over from the work on his
boat.

Even Benny stopped by once, happy as ever with Buffa
bouncing at the end of a new leash. He bragged that he had
found the monkey waiting for him at home the very day she
had run off. "Pretty smart she fin' her own way like dat,
huh?" said Benny. "Pretty smart," agreed Sammy, who knew
better than to suggest that Cosmo may have helped. Benny
also mentioned that he had ordered a new organ—"much
betta den de ol' one"—and would be working again within
the week.

Angelo came around a few times too. Earlier that day he
had even brought him a meatball sandwich for lunch. "Just
so's you don't forget to eat," he said. It was a gesture that
made Sammy feel special, like he was truly among friends.
But the feeling lasted only until Angelo started to leave.
Halfway up the ramp, he stopped and said, "Oh, maybe I
should have brought one for Cosmo too." And he laughed all
the way back to his restaurant.

Angelo's remark had ruined Sammy's appetite, and he was
busy sanding again when a shout rang out from above, "Eureka!
I found it!"

Sammy glanced up and saw Jenko standing at the top of
the ramp, looking like a pirate back from a looting spree. His
beard was wild and wind blown, his cane was stuck sword-

like under his belt, and he had five drip-stained paint cans raised triumphantly over his head.

Sammy threw down his sanding block and leaped out of the boat. He met the sculptor at the bottom of the ramp and helped him step down to the dock.

"Here," said Jenko, setting the paint at Sammy's feet. "You'd better see if this stuff is still good. I've had it on the shelf since I moved in. It's almost as old as you are."

Jenko sat down on the ramp and wiped his brow with a hanky while Sammy rummaged around for a screwdriver. He found one in the tool pile and pried off the rusted, crusted, airtight lids. He saw that none of the cans was more than half full, and the paint had thickened into cloudy globs of color topped by rubbery skins and an oily ooze.

"It looks pretty gooey," said Sammy.

"See if it stirs," suggested Jenko.

Sammy took a stick from the scrap pile and stuck it in the can of pink enamel. After churning a while, he said rather glumly, "It looks okay now."

"How much is there?"

"Enough for two coats, I guess."

Jenko sensed the tone of disappointment this time. "So what's the matter?"

"Well, they're not the greatest colors."

"Oh, no? What are they?"

Sammy peered into each can. "Pink, black, orange, green and purple," he said. "All yukky."

"What do you mean yukky? Everyone knows that pink, black, orange, green and purple are the only possible colors to paint a skiff."

"They do?"

"Of course."

"Then how come I've never seen one like that?"

"Because no one has ever had the courage to be first!"

"Oh," said Sammy, not quite convinced.

"Here, you'll need this too." Jenko pulled a paint brush out of his coat pocket and slid it across the dock toward Sammy. "And be sure to wash it out with Babe's turpentine before you change colors." Then Jenko stood up and drew his cane from his belt. "Let me check your preparations."

"I'm not finished yet," said Sammy.

But Jenko felt his way to the skiff anyway and ran his hands over the sides and gunnels. "Feels good to me," he said. "You sand much more and all you'll have left is a toy for your bathtub. It already must be the tiniest boat in the bay. How far out do we have to row anyway?"

"Just over the trench. No more than a mile."

"That's far enough. And it'd better be a calm night. If the wind's up, neither of us are going anywhere."

"You don't have to come if you're afraid. I can do it alone."

"Afraid! Why, I've crossed the equator more times than you've crossed your legs. You might not know it to look at me now, but I was an able-bodied seaman in my younger days. And I'll tell you a little secret, the first thing any good mate learns is to fear the sea."

"Is that why you gave it up?"

"No, no, no. You haven't been listening. Clean out your ears, I'll tell you why." And Jenko sang a few lines borrowed from an old chantey:

> *"The winds were foul, the ship was slow,*
> *So I left her, Sammy, I left her.*
> *The grub was bad and the wages low,*
> *So I just up and left her."*

He finished with a little jig, and then said, "Humph! 'Don't have to come if I'm afraid.' Where'd you get such a notion?"

Sammy dropped his head apologetically. "I only said that because I thought you were backing out."

"Not on your life. I know you'd go alone. But I'm holding you to your promise."

"What promise?"

"Yours and Cosmo's. You said you'd take me for a ride if I let you work out here, didn't you?"

"That's right, we did." Sammy smiled at the memory of those few hours when a skiff had made their universe complete. "You know," he sighed, "nobody else believes he's still around. I can tell they think I'm making it up."

"Well, I don't think that. I'll admit you're the first person I've met who says he's seen a ghost. But I'm perfectly willing to give you the benefit of the doubt. After all, I'm used to believing in things I can't see."

"I always wondered about that."

"What?"

Sammy stared into Jenko's gray eyes. "How you went blind?"

"Oh, that," Jenko chuckled. "No great tale there. I have what they call detached retinas. Those are the tissues in the back of the eye that absorb light. But mine tore loose and left me in the dark."

"How?"

"Well, it happened over a period of years. I hardly noticed at first. My right eye was always weak, but it never slowed me down. I was a good athlete in school and a promising artist too. Some of my paintings even won awards. And later I held down a full-time job at the Monterey Boat Works, building trawlers mostly. Your aunt was very sweet on me then."

"Really?"

"Oh, yes. And a beautiful girl she was, too. We were both

young and full of dreams. I still am, but at that time I wanted to be a famous painter and see the world. So I took my sketchbooks and went to sea.

"I was a merchant seaman for three-and-a-half years before my other eye acted up. It gave out while I was steaming through the Indian Ocean. We were somewhere between Fremantle and Yokohama with a hull full of iron ore. I remember being on the poop deck this one evening, leaning over the taffrail and enjoying the sunset, when things suddenly went blurry on me. Then all I could see were sparks, a snowstorm of sparks, shooting across my eye. When we made port, the captain took me to an ophthalmologist—that's an eye doctor—and he told me I'd never see again."

"What'd you do?"

"I went back to the ship and had a colossal cry. I was terrified. The greatest fear of my life was that I'd go blind, that I'd have to live in a world of darkness. To me the blind were all poor wretches, beggars on the bowery. I didn't want anyone's pity or charity. But I didn't know how I was going to support myself. And all my hopes and dreams as an artist were snuffed out. It was like a living death."

Sammy understood.

"I won't say I learned to accept it, because I never have. But after a couple of botched operations, I became resigned to the situation. I had to learn everything all over again: how to read with my fingers, walk with a cane, get dressed so that my socks match, cook a meal without burning or poisoning myself—all of that. I couldn't paint anymore, of course, but I discovered sculpting. I started working with clay, and then wood and stone. I love it, and now it even pays the rent!"

"Is everything all black?" asked Sammy.

"Yes, but I can still see with these." Jenko raised his hands. "And my hearing is keener than sonar," he said, pulling his left ear. "My sense of smell and taste ain't so bad either," he added, patting his round belly. Then he laughed.

"But enough of that. It's time for me to shove off." Jenko slapped the side of the boat. "Be sure to wipe her down with a rag before you put on the undercoat."

Sammy said okay and looked once more into the cans; into the thick, gooey pools of pink, black, orange, green and purple — the "yukky" colors Jenko would never see.

CHAPTER NINE
A Grave Encounter

SAMMY SQUIRMED in the pew. His gray slacks had never been itchier and his bow tie felt like a noose around his neck. Even his feet seemed to be suffocating in Cosmo's pointy dress shoes.

He was in church, of course, the Mission San Carlos, and he could hardly stand it. The place was dark as a cave, and so stuffy he thought he was going to throw up. Luckily Aunt Nastina didn't come too often, for this was his usual reaction to Sunday Mass. Sammy always found the heavy, incense-ladened air of the church impossible to breathe, even without a cinched windpipe.

He pulled at his collar and wriggled his toes so they wouldn't be permanently damaged, but Aunt Nastina nudged him again with her missal. "Keep still!" she whispered out of the side of her mouth. She kept her eyes fixed on the monsignor, a red-faced Irishman in rimless glasses and bright green vestments. He was preaching up in the pulpit, a kind of crow's nest built onto the west wall and suspended over the front pews.

Sammy tried to pay attention to his sermon. After all, it was the only part of the Mass not in Latin. But he couldn't figure out why the guy was so mad; why he kept yelling at the people and pointing his finger at them, as if he were scolding a bunch of children.

The priest was actually his own worst distraction. He had a frothy brogue, and the louder he sermonized and the farther he leaned out over his congregation, the more spittle would form in the corners of his mouth. Sammy watched a while to see if it would drip down on some poor soul. But it never did and he got bored with the game. If Cosmo had been there, they probably wouldn't have been able to stop laughing. But without him, the service was insufferable.

All Sammy wanted to do was finish painting the skiff. He couldn't help thinking that he might even have been done by now if Aunt Nastina hadn't nabbed him on his way out the door this morning. "Oh, no you don't," she had said. "Get out of those paint clothes. You're coming to Mass with me."

"But, Auntie . . . "

"Don't 'But Auntie' me. It's time you said some prayers for your brother. Help his soul out of purgatory. Not that I'm one to pass judgment, but you know good and well a scamp like that couldn't have made it to heaven right off. Besides, people will expect to see you there."

Sammy tried to explain how he was allergic to church, but Aunt Nastina wouldn't listen. She made him dress up and walk with her the seven blocks to the mission. They reached the courtyard gate just as the bells in the tower started ringing, and Aunt Nastina stopped to place a black lace veil on her head.

On their way in, they nodded hello to Angelo and the other Italian men who always stood outside the open doors, too proud to enter and kneel, yet too God-fearing to miss Mass altogether. Sammy wanted to stay in the back with them, but he and Aunt Nastina were ushered right up front.

The ceiling of the church was high, and their footsteps echoed off the flagstones as they walked down the center aisle. The only light inside was that which came through the rear doors, the few stained-glass windows, or from the long, white candles on the altar.

Behind the altar loomed a life-sized crucifix, upon which was a Jesus whose left toes had been kissed away by the faithful. Various martyrs and madonnas were depicted in paintings around the church, and an array of saints were perched in niches in the walls. The most prominent of these statues was of Santa Rosalia, protectress of the fleet. She was portrayed as a young beauty holding a skull, which Sammy took to mean that even she believed in Halloween as a night of extraordinary power.

A choir of infants squalled throughout the Mass, either solo or in unison. Their parents tried to rock and whisper them into quietude, but usually to no avail. In fact, the screamers seemed to save their sharpest notes for the monsignor's sermon. He was used to the competition, however, and a few well-focused frowns forced some fathers to hustle their bawling babes outside.

After the sermon, the priest returned to the altar for the second half of the Mass, at which point baskets were passed around for the collection. Aunt Nastina dug into her purse and pulled out a ten dollar bill. She made a grand gesture of handing it to Sammy to toss in, which he did, wondering if it wasn't his own money he was parting with.

To pass the rest of the time, he watched the altar boy. He was a skinny-faced kid who looked familiar, even in his long black cassock and blousy white surplice. The boy puttered around in reverent attendance to the monsignor. But Sammy thought it was a silly waste of time when he brought the priest a bowl of water and a towel to wash his hands. Why on earth couldn't the guy have washed up before Mass, he wondered.

And still the service dragged on and on. The monsignor kept babbling away in Latin. The choir in the loft kept intoning "Amens" and "Hosannas." And everyone else kept standing and kneeling, standing and kneeling.

When time came for Communion, and people started filing up to kneel along the altar rail, Sammy's spirits rose, for it meant that Mass was almost over. But then someone appeared that made him do a double take. Out of the sacristy came another priest, and following him was the big red-headed kid.

Sammy couldn't believe his eyes. The redhead had on the same angelic garb as the other altar boy and held a golden tray against his breast. How could they let him up there? Didn't they know the kinds of things he did? Didn't they.... Now Sammy recognized the other boy! He was the redhead's sidekick, the one who lit the bomb that killed the seagull.

That did it. Sammy made up his mind never to set foot in church again. As long as he lived. No matter what Aunt Nastina said. Just then, she tapped him on the shoulder. "Watch my purse," she said as she slipped past him and cut into line.

Sammy stood up on the kneeler to get a clearer view of the two-faced bully. He saw that he was helping the priest hand out Communion. They slid along the rail together, the priest laying the Hosts on people's tongues, and the redhead holding the tray under their chins in case one fell. His eyes and manner reflected a seriousness that disgusted Sammy. He wondered how the kid could be so concerned about keeping a little piece of bread from hitting the floor, yet not even care that he caused Cosmo to fall, caused him to die.

Sammy started shaking, the anger in him rising to a boil. He gripped the pew in front to steady himself. But he still felt wobbly, flushed, short of breath. He yanked off his tie, popping the top button of his shirt. He heard it bouncing on the flagstones and saw people staring at him, but he didn't care. He pushed past them out of the pew and, without even pretending to genuflect, bolted up the aisle.

Angelo and the others were still basking in the sunlit courtyard when Sammy staggered out of the church.

"What's the matter?" Angelo asked. "You see the Holy Ghost?"

"That's not funny!" Sammy yelled back at him. He stalked out the gates and sat down on the curb. Angelo just shrugged to his friends and circled his finger by his ear to signify the boy was *pazzo* — crazy.

Sammy soon heard the strains of the closing hymn surging from the church. A minute later he looked back and saw the altar boys and the monsignor emerge single file from the dark tunnel-like interior. They each dropped their folded hands as they crossed the threshold.

The boys headed around the corner of the church, but the priest called them back and handed them a few of his outer vestments. Standing now in a plain white robe, he greeted his parishoners as they came out of the church.

The redhead and his partner, each loaded down with the clothes but giddy after the solemn hour, skipped off again toward the sacristy. Sammy sneered at them, wishing he had the power of the Evil Eye, the power to trip them up, or turn them into skeletons, or something.

At that moment, the redhead looked back across the courtyard. He stopped dead in his tracks when he spotted Sammy. The grin fell instantly from his round, freckled face. He stood frozen like that for a few seconds, a few skipped heartbeats, and then hurried off after his friend.

The courtyard was suddenly swarming with church-goers. They engulfed Sammy as they poured out the gate and headed for their cars. When most had passed, Sammy looked back again and saw Aunt Nastina talking to the monsignor. He decided to go up to them, thinking that she couldn't get as mad with a priest present.

"This must be the lad right here," said the monsignor as Sammy approached.

Aunt Nastina glared at her nephew. "I can't get over you," she said. "Won't you even allow me an hour's peace on a Sunday morning? What do you mean by taking off like that, leaving my purse unattended?"

"I thought I was going to be sick," said Sammy. "I was afraid I'd throw up in there."

"I don't want to hear that allergic-to-church routine anymore," Aunt Nastina replied.

"Perhaps it would help if he came a bit more regularly," said the monsignor, eyeing Aunt Nastina reproachfully. Then he looked down kindly at Sammy. "Top o' the mornin', son. I'm Monsignor O'Casey. I understand ye've had a hard time of late. Comes as no surprise, no surprise. It's a terrible thing to lose a brother. I'll bet ye looked up to him like a prince."

Sammy shrugged. He saw there was no more foaminess in the corners of the priest's mouth.

"D'ye know it was I who celebrated his Requiem Mass?" the monsignor continued. "Ye weren't there, were ye? A pity. I wish now I'd've stopped by the house to see ye afterwards."

"Yeah, we celebrated there too," said Sammy.

Monsignor O'Casey nodded without understanding. Then he bent over and said, "I hope you're afeelin' free to come here any time ye want. It can be a great comfort to say a few prayers on a loved one's grave."

"What grave?" asked Sammy.

The priest looked aghast at Aunt Nastina, who quickly came to her own defense. "I thought it was much too early to put him through that," she said. "Graveyards can be very disturbing to children."

"Aye, an' to some adults," shot back the monsignor. Then he turned to Sammy and said, "Cosmo's buried in the back. Why don't we walk over and say a wee prayer for him?"

"Oh, Monsignor, do you really think it wise?" cut in Aunt Nastina.

"A grave's as common as a cradle, woman, and we've no cause to be afraid of either."

He took Sammy's hand and led him around the corner. They walked briskly down a stone path, passed under an adobe arch, and halted there at the entrance to the cemetery. It was a narrow garden of headstones and crosses tucked between the rear of the church and the courtyard wall. A splendid pepper tree grew in the center, shading the nearest graves. They were laid out in rows, one oblong hump of earth after another; some ringed with abalone shells, others carpeted with ice plant.

When Aunt Nastina caught up to Sammy and the monsignor, they all proceeded to the grave in the far corner that was surrounded by wilting wreaths.

"Here we are," said the priest. "A fine spot, don't ye think? Plenty of mornin' sun."

Sammy wondered why that mattered. He inhaled the perfumey stink of the flowers and noticed the colorful petals that had fallen onto the dirt. He pictured the coffin just below the surface, yet felt strangely unmoved, even when he read the white stone marker:

COSMO SERAFINO

1943–1955

"Shall we bow our heads an' pray?" said the monsignor. Sammy watched as the priest closed his eyes and began:

"Dear Lord, here lies thy young servant, Cosmo. He was our brother an' we miss him dearly. We come now to ask for the Christian fortitude to remember that the separation o' death is not final for those who believe in yer limitless love. We beseech thy divine mercy on his immortal soul, an' all the souls o' the faithful departed. *Requiem aeternam dona eis, Domine.* Eternal rest grant unto them, O Lord. Amen."

Monsignor O'Casey looked over the top of his glasses at Sammy and said, "Would ye like to add a few words o' yer own?"

Sammy shook his head no.

"Go on, son," he urged. "Just tell him ye love him an' are akeepin' him in yer prayers."

"He's not there," said Sammy.

"Sammy!" cried Aunt Nastina.

"No, no, the lad's quite right. He knows his catechism," said the monsignor. He bowed his head again and prayed: "An' Lord, though our brother's untimely departure has left us most distraught, we take heart in knowin' that his soul has entered the Celestial Kingdom, an' that he is asittin' beside thee now. We thank thee for grantin' him life everlastin', an' may he watch over us with all the other saints an' angels in heaven."

The monsignor looked once more at Sammy, who was shaking his head no. "He's not there either," said Sammy. "He's under the wharf."

"Sammy, please!" cried Aunt Nastina. "Don't start that again."

"What are ye sayin', son?"

"He's a ghost. I've seen him."

Aunt Nastina threw up her hands.

"Go on, tell me more," urged the monsignor. "When'd ye see him? And where?"

"The first time was in our shed, a day or two after the funeral party. The other time was last week when I was working in the storeroom. That's the day we went over to Angelo's and got into a little trouble. He hasn't changed much, you know."

"What does he look like?"

"Same as always, only kind of light and airy. And he's wearing a white tuxedo, but no shoes. They cheated him out of shoes."

"Is that right? 'As he spoken to ye?"

"Oh, sure."

"What'd he have to say?"

"Lots of things, but mostly he said it wasn't my fault he died, and that my being sad was weighing him down."

"Very interesting!" said the monsignor. "You know, the Irish believe that it's unwise to mourn anyone too long, lest they be kept from their rest an' return as a ghost. It's partly why we tend to have such lively wakes."

Aunt Nastina interrupted, "I've heard enought of this morbid mumbo-jumbo. Let's get going."

The monsignor frowned at her. Then he said to Sammy, "I don't doubt ye've see'n somethin', lad, but have ye considered it might just be a figment o' yer imagination?"

"He's here all right," said Sammy. "But it's okay if you don't believe me. Hardly anyone does."

"No, no, I didn't say that. Ye forget I come from the Land o' the Little People—leprechauns, water sheeries, and all manner of ghosts an' fairy folk. Such spirits have haunted the Irish countryside, or at least the minds o' the peasantry, since time immemorial."

"Really?"

"Aye, so what else did yer ghost say?"

"Well, he said he couldn't leave the wharf for a hundred years unless I helped him. That's why I've been fixing up our skiff to start him off. It's almost ready."

"A wee voyage, ye say? Sounds like an adventure on the order of our own Saint Brendan's. Ye know about him, don't ye?"

"No."

"I'm surprised. He was the intrepid seaman missionary o' the Middle Ages. Irish, o' course. He an' his monks sailed all over the Emerald Isles — an' beyond — in oxhide coracles. He's even reputed t'ave sailed to America before Columbus."

"Who didn't?" replied Sammy.

Monsignor O'Casey looked puzzled. "Well, never mind about that," he said. "But tell me, how far will ye be going?"

"Just over the trench," said Sammy. "We need deep water." The priest knitted his brow in concern. Sammy quickly added, "Don't worry, Cosmo has it all worked out. He's learning a magic rhyme to rise with the tide. The moon'll be full tomorrow, you know."

"Tomorrow! Why, that's different. That's All Hallow's Eve, a most propitious time for souls to be liberated!"

"Please!" wailed Aunt Nastina. "Don't encourage him!"

"It is?" said Sammy.

"Aye, the ancient Celts regarded it as their New Year's Day, the beginnin' o' winter, an' a time when the year's dead flocked back to mingle with the living. Villagers held great festivals. They dressed in animal skins and lit bonfires on the hillsides, offerin' gifts and sacrifices so the souls could be freed to claim their heavenly reward."

"How could you fill his head with such nonsense?" demanded Aunt Nastina.

"Nonsense? That's history! Those festivals were made a

part o' the Church calendar. What d'ye think All Souls' Day is? The day we pray specially for the dead in the hope o' speedin' their stay in purgatory. An' why d'ye think it comes right on the heels o' Halloween? 'Cause it was a time people already associated with the throngin' o' spirits."

"Humph!" snorted Aunt Nastina, with her nose in the air. "Sammy, it's time to go. I have a shop to open." And she marched off in a huff. Sammy and the monsignor shrugged at each other and then slowly followed.

"Ye must admit," said the priest as they walked, "ghosts have lost a bit o' their credibility in this day and age. Perhaps for the best, but still one never knows about the supernatural; the Lord works in mysterious ways."

Sammy nodded. They passed under the adobe arch, and the priest stopped. When Sammy looked back, Monsignor O'Casey waved and shouted, "Hail and farewell, lad."

CHAPTER TEN
Moonseeker

THERE," SAID SAMMY, "finished!"

It was now late afternoon and he was standing on Jenko's dock with paint brush in hand, admiring his artistry. The skiff, still up on sawhorses, glistened before him. She was the brightest, gayest colored boat he had ever seen. The sides were pink with green trim, the hull was purple, the thwarts and gunnels black, and the inside orange. It was his own design and he thought it fabulous.

"What d'ya think?"

He turned to old Gao, who was sitting on the edge of the ramp smoking a cigarette. Gao had on his familiar wide-brimmed cowboy hat, but he had left his shoulder pole at home, for Sunday was his one day off.

"I think you got more paint on yourself than on the boat," Gao said.

Sammy looked down at his hands and clothes. They were indeed smeared and splattered with all five colors, plus a few splotches of roofing tar. The pants, sneakers and sweatshirt he had changed into after church were the same ones he had worn all week because Aunt Nastina didn't want him to ruin any others. What Sammy couldn't see without a mirror, though, was that today even his face and hair were streaked with paint.

"Oh, well," he said, "Jenko told me not to be stingy with the stuff."

"I only joking," said Gao. "The boat look good. You just better hope fish don't get scared off by all those color."

"Oh, no," said Sammy. "I bet fish will like it."

Sammy walked over to where his supplies were spread out on sheets of newspaper. He kneeled down and swished his brush in the coffee can now filled with Babe's murky turpentine. Then he noticed the can with the little bit of black paint left in it. "There's just one more thing to do," he said.

"What?" asked Gao.

"Name her."

"Name who?"

"The skiff! Who d'ya think?"

Gao screwed up his face. "Nobody names skiffs," he said. "They too small; they don't need names."

"This one does," said Sammy.

Gao shrugged. "Go ahead then."

"I would if I could think of something good enough," sighed Sammy as he pressed the bristles clean. "It has to be just right." He stood up and shook out the brush. Then he tossed it on the newspaper and reached for the rag in his back pocket. As he pulled it out, the torn, dog-eared photograph of his parents fell face-down onto the dock. Gao saw it and was about to say something when Sammy's face lit up like sun on a window. "I got an idea!" he shouted. "Why don't you name her?"

"Me?" said Gao, pointing to his nose.

"Yeah," said Sammy. "We're partners, aren't we? I want you to name her. Anything you want. Even a Chinese name."

"Bah!" said Gao, throwing his cigarette butt in the water.

"Ahoy there!" came a shout from atop the ramp. Sammy

and Gao looked up and saw Jenko and his actress friend, the one who had played Queen Isabella. Both were dressed in shorts, sandals, and pullovers, and the actress carried a large straw basket. They descended the ramp together, with Jenko holding onto her elbow.

"I thought we'd find you here," said Jenko. "We just got back from a romantic picnic in the hills. What a view! Heh, heh. How's the work coming?"

"Good," said Sammy. "I just finished painting. So you can't touch."

"Can't touch? That's what I've been hearing all day!"

The actress slapped Jenko's arm playfully. He covered up like a boxer and they both laughed.

"Don't listen to him," said the actress. "Your boat looks wonderful. Such festive colors!"

"Thanks," said Sammy.

"And I love your matching face," she teased. "With all that paint, you certainly won't need a mask to go trick-or-treating tomorrow."

Sammy touched his cheek, but only rubbed on more paint.

"Oh, no!" laughed the actress, "You're making it worse!"

Sammy looked down in embarrassment. "It'll come off with turpentine," he mumbled.

"You need turpentine shampoo, too," added Gao.

"Who's that?" asked Jenko, cocking his head.

"It's old Gao," said Sammy. "He's been keeping me company. We're partners."

"Well, how do you do, sir?" said Jenko. "It's a pleasure to finally meet you." He turned to the actress. "Mr. Gao is a living legend in this town. He's a direct descendent of Monterey Bay's first fishing family."

Gao waved off Jenko's intended flattery. "No living legend," he said. "Just old man who won't go away. You famous one in town, famous artist ever since you were boy."

"Gao liked your Columbus statue a lot," Sammy interjected, "even though he doesn't care much for Columbus."

"Well, I'm glad somebody liked it," said Jenko. "May they both rest in peace."

Sammy saw Gao was confused and he explained, "It got stolen, you know."

"Yes, yes," said Jenko. "But Western Civilization will survive the loss, and so will I. So tell me, Sammy. Are we all set for tomorrow night?"

"All set," he answered. "The paint should be dry by the afternoon and I'll put her in the water then."

"And we have your aunt's permission, right?"

"'Course."

"Okay, then. When shall we meet?"

"It'll take about an hour to row out, don't you think? How about ten-thirty here on the dock?"

"Fine, fine. And I'll bring my alarm clock so we'll know exactly when it's midnight."

"Where are you going?" asked the actress.

"Oh, just for a little bay cruise," said Jenko.

"At night?" said Gao. "That crazy. No good bottom fishing at night."

"We're not going fishing," said Sammy. "But don't worry, when I do you'll get first dibs on everything."

"I don't worry 'bout that," said Gao. "I just know it dangerous to row boat when you can't even see the end of your oars."

Sammy's face turned livid, as if he had suddenly become seasick. "Oh, no," he said. "I forgot all about that. We don't have any oars." He wheeled around toward Jenko. "But you can make us some, can't you?"

"Oars? Now?" said Jenko. "Why didn't you say something earlier?"

"You gotta do it!" begged Sammy.

"There's not enough time," said Jenko. "Why don't we just borrow a pair from one of the other skiffs tied up here? I'm sure no one would mind."

Sammy ran to the edge of the dock and jumped into the nearest skiff. He pulled up a set of oars from beneath the thwarts, but they had a chain linked through holes in the paddle end. He threw them down and jumped into the neighboring boat. But its oars were chained too. So he leaped into the next skiff, and the next one, until they all were rocking and banging as though a speed boat had passed by. Even the dock was bobbing so much that the actress had to hold onto the squeaking ramp.

Finally, Sammy cried out, "It's no good. They're all chained up."

"Just buy some at Hooper's tomorrow." hollered Gao.

"With what?" Sammy shouted back. "I don't even have the money you lent me." He slumped down on the thwart like a washed-up jellyfish. "Now we'll never get out," he pouted.

"Wait a minute," said the actress. "I know where we can get a pair. At the theatre! There's a row boat in the third act of *Anchors Aweigh*. It's only a cardboard prop, but the oars are real. They're brand new. Too new! I'll tell the manager they need some weathering to look more authentic. He'll let me borrow them. There's no show till Friday. Wait here." She handed Jenko the basket and whisked up the ramp.

"You can rest easy, Sammy," assured Jenko. "She'll come through for you."

"I hope so," he replied. "I don't know how I forgot about the oars."

The three of them stood there in silence until Jenko said,

"Well, you may as well start cleaning up. How are my tools? Did you put them where I told you?"

"All except the brush," said Sammy. "I wanted to wait until I painted the name on the bow."

"Oh, right," said Jenko. "What are you going to name her?"

"I don't know yet. Gao was going to help me, weren't you?"

Gao got up muttering in Chinese. He went over and picked up Sammy's photograph. "This is yours," he said.

Sammy jumped up and felt his back pocket. "Where'd you get that?" he yelled.

"What you think, I steal it? It fell out your pocket."

"Oh," said Sammy. He pulled the chain of the skiff he was in until it floated close enough for him to jump back onto the dock.

Meanwhile, Gao studied the photo. "It's a picture of your father and mother, isn't it?" he asked. "They look just like you. Was that their sailboat?"

"Yeah," said Sammy, now on the dock. "It's the one that sank."

"Ah, yes," said Jenko. "They loved the sea too. It must be in the blood."

"What they call that boat?" Gao asked.

"I forget," said Sammy. "I was just a kid then."

"What you mean you forget?" barked Gao. "You can almost read it in the picture. Here, your eyes better than mine. What that say on the hull, *Moonsex?*" He handed the photo to Sammy.

"No," he said. "I remember now. They're standing in front of the last part. That's *Moonseeker.*"

"*Moonseeker!*" exclaimed Jenko. "Now there's a fitting name."

"Good enough for little skiff," said Gao.

"You think so?" said Sammy. "Wouldn't it be bad luck, seeing how the first one went down?"

"No," said Gao. "It good luck to carry on ancestral name. Ups and downs part of life."

"All right, then," said Sammy. "*Moonseeker* it is!"

"Perfect!" said Jenko. "Your aunt will hate it. Paint it on right now." He opened the basket and felt around carefully until he pulled out a paring knife. "Here, take this and cut the name in block letters on some newspaper. That'll be your stencil."

"I don't print so good," said Sammy. "You do it, Gao. Please?"

Gao grumbled again, but took the knife from Jenko.

Half an hour later, just as Sammy and Gao had finished painting the name on both sides of the bow, the actress came bouncing down the ramp. Slung over her shoulder were two wooden oars, complete with clanking metal locks. She marched straight to Sammy and handed them to him, saying:

"Here you are, Admiral. Consider it a loan from Her Highness, Queen Isabella."

Sammy, smiling joyously and recalling Cosmo's gesture, thanked her with a regal bow.

That night, after a tasty supper and a hot snooze-inducing bath, Sammy bid his aunt good night and padded up to bed in his pajamas and slippers. At the top of the stairs he noticed a wedge of soft light coming through the crack of the door. Pushing it open, he beheld the gleaming white moon peering through his window. It hovered just above the horizon, and already looked magnificently full.

Sammy went over to the window and gazed upon the luminous sphere as if for the first time. He studied its mottled surface and could almost feel its magnetic quality. He smiled at the thought of Cosmo sailing upwards, but it soon saddened him. He realized that after tomorrow he would never see his brother again in any form. He knew he would miss Cosmo, but he was more worried that he would forget him, just as he had forgotten so much about his parents. He feared that someday he wouldn't be able to recall Cosmo's dumb smirk, or how he could run across a wobbly plank, or the way his hair smelled when they wrestled.

Sammy sighed deeply and looked over at the oars laid across Cosmo's bed. He wondered what Coz would do if he couldn't leave, if something went wrong; if there was a storm, say, or if Aunt Nastina made him take a nap and he slept past midnight. Cosmo'd be mad, sure, but he'd get over it, figured Sammy. Then he shook his head. "No," he said aloud. "He'd never forgive me."

CHAPTER ELEVEN
Red's Return

HE SHOULD HAVE KNOWN right then it would be a day of rocky comings and goings.

Sammy had slept late for the first time in weeks, and it was almost noon when he awoke, threw on fresh clothes, and dashed out the door with the oars tucked under his arm.

Unfortunately, however, Aunt Nastina was returning for lunch just then and they collided on the back porch. He fell on his rear-end, she did a screaming cartwheel in the air and landed on top of him, and the oars slid thwak-thwak-thwak down the steps.

"What in the world . . . " shrieked Aunt Nastina, her knobby knees poking out of the blue ruffles of her dress. "Why don't you watch where you're going? You could have killed me with those things!" Her left stocking had a wicked run in it and her hair was all mussed.

"I . . . I'm sorry," stammered her squashed nephew. "I didn't see you."

"Well open your eyes next time!"

Sammy slipped out from under her and climbed to his feet. He offered a hand to his aunt, but she slapped it away and used the railing to pull herself up.

"Ughhh!" she moaned. "I'm going to be bruised all over. Where were you going in such a hurry anyway?"

"Just down to launch my skiff. She's still up on sawhorses."

"The skiff! Always the skiff! When are you going to get over that nonsense? Abner and his psychology. . . . "

"Huh?"

"Never mind. Just tell me where you got those paddles. That's what I'd like to know."

"They're oars. A friend lent them to me."

"Who?"

"Jenko's friend, the lady that's in all the plays."

"That floozy? Why doesn't she mind her own business?"

"She was trying to help; I need them."

"Humph," snorted Aunt Nastina. "Come inside, it's time for lunch."

"I'm not hungry."

Aunt Nastina scowled suspiciously. "Wait a minute," she said. "You're not supposed to go out in that thing until late tonight. Isn't that the plan?"

"Yeah, with Jenko."

"All right then, I don't want you trying it out on your own beforehand. And listen, I'm expecting a big delivery this afternoon, so I'm going to want you to help me stock shelves after dinner."

"But it's Hallo—"

"I don't want to hear any 'buts' about it. After all the days I've let you waste on that boat, you can certainly give me a few hours."

"Okay," Sammy agreed reluctantly. "Just for a while, though." He walked down the stairs and picked up the oars.

"Meantime, keep those clothes clean," admonished his aunt.

Sammy nodded and as he rounded the shop's corner, he heard her holler another familiar order: "And don't go under the wharf!"

Despite the nasty head-on collision, Sammy skipped down the pier in the highest of spirits. It was business as usual, with tourists strolling about, merchants hawking their wares, and seagulls wheeling overhead. Sammy greeted everyone he passed. He waved hello to Benny and Buffa, who were entertaining a crowd with their new organ. He saluted Sergeant Abner, who was making his midday rounds. And he shouted "Happy Halloween!" to Ratzo and his wife. They all waved back, surprised to see him in such good cheer again.

"AYE–Aye-aye-aye . . . "

An incredible cacophony of shrieking seagulls rang out as Sammy approached Jenko's dock. Their ear-splitting cries made him think the entire bird world was rioting. On reaching the ramp, he saw a tornado of gulls whirling above the *Moonseeker.* And standing inside her, in the funnel of the screeching twister, was the big redheaded kid. He held a loaf of French bread under his arm and was tearing off chunks and throwing them up to the birds.

A gush of fear and anger swept through Sammy. He swallowed dryly and considered coming back later. But he couldn't just skulk away and leave that guy standing in his boat. Not now. Not after working so hard. Not even if it meant getting beat up. Sammy swung the oars over his shoulder and held them like weapons at the ready. He knew there was no avoiding a showdown.

"Get outa there!" yelled Sammy. But the redhead didn't hear him amid the frenzy of feasting seagulls. So Sammy shouted again even louder, "I said get outa my boat!"

The redhead looked up this time. He didn't seem at all surprised to see it was Sammy. He merely tossed the rest of the loaf in the water, and sat down to watch the birds swarm around it.

Sammy mustered his courage and marched down the ramp.

He stopped at the *Moonseeker's* colorful bow and said, "This is private property. You've got no business here."

"I'm not hurtin' anything," answered the redhead, still watching the birds. He was dressed in brown corduroys and a white shirt half untucked under a green sweater. Sammy recognized it as the uniform of the mission school.

"You're in my boat!" he yelled.

The kid looked around at the skiff as if he hadn't noticed it before. "Where'd you get this?" he asked.

"None of your business," said Sammy. He set down one oar and hefted the other one clobber-level. "Now get out."

"I didn't come to pick on you," said the redhead.

"Then what do you want?"

"Nothing."

"Yes you do."

All was silent except for the whining of the gulls. Then the redhead blurted out, "I came to say I'm sorry. About your brother, I mean."

Sammy was unmoved. "As if you really care."

"I do. I didn't mean for him to fall. None of us did. We just wanted the firecrackers back."

"It's still your fault, no matter what you say," replied Sammy. "Cosmo wouldn't have bothered you if you hadn't killed that seagull."

The redhead looked down in shame. "I'm sorry about the bird too," he said. "I don't know why I did it. I felt really bad afterwards."

"You're a liar. I saw you all laughing."

"That's because I wanted the guys to think it was neat. It didn't start bugging me 'til later. It got so bad I couldn't even look at a gull in the air without seeing it explode. And they followed me everywhere." The boy paused and looked up at Sammy. "Same with that statue."

"Huh?

"That statue of your brother. I kept seeing it all the time, like in the curtains at night. I couldn't stand it. That's why . . . that's why I rolled it off the wharf."

"You what?"

"I came back one night and rolled it off the wharf."

Sammy glared at the redhead with undisguised disgust.

"I'm sorry," the kid blubbered. "I didn't know what else to do. It wouldn't leave me alone." He began bawling and his freckled, tear-streaked face scrunched uglier with each sob.

"You . . . you . . . " Sammy couldn't find the words to vent his rage. In his frustration he swung the oar full force at the redhead and it whooshed just over his head. The kid jumped back in alarm.

"I hate you," said Sammy. "I hate your guts." And he took another wild swipe at the guy. This time the oar struck him squarely on the shoulder, knocking him over the center thwart. The force of his fall jerked the skiff backwards. The bow slid off the front sawhorse, the rear horse buckled, and the boat crashed hard against the dock.

"Look what you did!" screamed Sammy. "I told you to get out of there!"

"Don't hit me anymore," cried the redhead. "Don't hit me anymore."

The oar felt heavy in Sammy's hand and he let it slip to the dock. He wanted to cry himself now, not over his fallen skiff, but over the destructiveness of his anger and guilt.

The redhead picked himself up. "You can hate me; I don't blame you. But the gulls have forgiven me. I know they have."

Sammy looked at the seagulls staring down hungrily from the roofs and railings. He didn't think birds remembered well enough to forgive. But he began to see how pointless it was to ease grief with hatred, to blame anyone—even himself—for Cosmo's death.

"Why don't you just go," he whispered hoarsely. "Help me get this boat in the water and then go, okay?"

The kid rubbed his sore shoulder. "All right," he said. He climbed out of the skiff and Sammy went over to see if there was any damage. Everything looked okay. So while the red-head moved the sawhorses and kicked the old coffee can out of the way, Sammy tied a line of mismatched ropes through the ring in the bow. He then directed the redhead to the opposite side.

"Ready . . . lift!" he said, and they carried the boat over to the dock's edge. They set it down gently, switched their grips, and slid it off. POOSH! It hit the water with a clean splash. Sammy, having kept hold of the line, now tied it to a cleat. Then he stood up to admire his craft, which floated high and fine.

"Looks great," said the redhead.

Sammy nodded.

"You gonna try it out now? I'll go with you."

"I don't think so," said Sammy.

The redhead sighed, and his disappointment filled the silence that followed. After standing at the edge a while, he said, "Well, I guess I better get back to school."

He was halfway up the ramp when Sammy suddenly wheeled around. "Hey," he called out, "what's your name, anyway?"

The kid stopped and smiled hopefully. "Randy," he replied, "but my friends call me Red."

CHAPTER TWELVE
Halloween Horrors

THIS IS NOTHING but a night of mischief," said Aunt Nastina. "I'll be glad when it's over."

"Me too," Sammy agreed, though for different reasons.

They were standing in the darkened entrance of the gift shop. Aunt Nastina was digging through her purse for the keys to unlock the door, while Sammy marveled at the multitude of masked characters converging on the wharf.

There were ghosts and gorillas, mummies and mobsters, pirates and princesses, vikings and vampires, all laughing and carrying on as though transformed by their costumes. They weren't kids out trick-or-treating, but adults going to the Halloween party at Angelo's. Sammy recalled what the priest had told him about the ancient customs of the night, and now saw these people as they were—actors in a cosmic ritual.

He looked up. The night was cool and clear except for a high ceiling of fog, which barely filtered the moon's brightness. He couldn't see the burning globe, but he knew it was there in all its fullness. He knew because he had watched it throughout the day while lolling in his skiff, waiting for the hours to drift by. He had never noticed the moon in the afternoon before, and he couldn't get over how pale and misplaced it looked, like a little soul in limbo. He had been glad when dusk finally settled.

"Let's go," said Aunt Nastina, pushing open the door.

The shop was alive with shadows. A single night light behind the cash register glowed eerily in all the mirrors and windows, making each piece of merchandise appear as a mere spectre of itself. The most ominous of these were the twin suits of armor silhouetted against the front wall. They somehow seemed angry at having been born into the wrong century.

Ticking tensely at the end of each aisle were the four grandfather clocks. Their unsynchronized heartbeats sounded to Sammy like warnings from another dimension. He tried to ignore them as he followed his aunt toward the storeroom, his hands pressed against his sides.

All at once, in spiteful unison, the clocks proclaimed the hour. They CHIMED! and GONGED! and DINGED! and DONGED!—eight times each, scaring Sammy silly. Then they dozed off again, like the sleepy old men they resembled.

"When'll we be done here?" Sammy asked afterwards.

"Soon," said Aunt Nastina.

"Before ten?"

"Long before."

"Good."

Despite the fright and his initial misgivings, Sammy was not unhappy to be helping his aunt. It had occurred to him that afternoon, while sunning himself in the skiff, that working late would be just the thing to keep from falling asleep and missing the rendezvous.

He was surprised, however, when Aunt Nastina unlocked the storeroom door and pushed him in ahead of her. She must be afraid of the dark, he reasoned.

The long, narrow room was black as a coffin. Sammy couldn't see a thing, but he bravely felt his way down the steps. Suddenly the overhead lights flicked on and he shielded his dazzled eyeballs with both arms.

When his eyes finally adjusted and he looked around, he saw that the storeroom was neater and cleaner than ever. There were no new boxes anywhere. He turned toward his aunt, who was standing with her back to the door. "Where's the..." But the answer came to him before he finished. There had been no delivery. It was just a trick to lure him there.

"You lied," he said in a shocked whisper.

"I'm sorry," said Nastina, "but there's no way I'm letting you out on that bay with a foolish old blind man."

"But you have to," said Sammy. "You promised!"

"I promised nothing of the kind. All I said was that you could work on the boat. You assumed the rest."

"That's not fair," argued Sammy. "That's not what you said."

"Life's not fair," she declared, backing out the door.

"You don't understand," he shrieked. "Cosmo needs me!"

"I understand plenty. You're staying right here until twelve. If your ghost can't find his way home by himself, then too bad."

"Too bad yourself," muttered Sammy as he rushed past her.

"Oh, no you don't," she said, catching him by the collar and swinging him back inside. Then she smacked his mouth with the back of her hand. "And that's for sassing me!"

Sammy collapsed crying on the top step. When he looked up moments later, he saw Aunt Nastina watching him through the crack of the door. She had a pained expression on her face. "I'm sorry," she said again, and closed the door. Sammy heard the key turn in the lock and the dead bolt fall into place.

"Auntie, no!" He lunged at the door and started beating on it. "Let me out! Let me out!" he cried, until his sob-choked voice went hoarse and he had pounded his little fists numb.

An hour later, when the clocks struck again, Sammy still lay slumped and spent against the door. His eyes were stinging red and his cheeks streaked with the salt of tears. Aunt Nastina's betrayal had left him in a stupor of self-pity.

But his courage returned as he listened to the muffled chimes and gongs on the other side of the door. They roused his sense of duty and reminded him of the urgency of his task. Slowly, he rose to his feet.

Sammy studied the room anew, determined to escape. He wasted no time regretting the absence of windows, but focused on the back door. It was still barricaded with boxes. They were stacked almost to the ceiling, two and three rows deep. Only one corner of the door was exposed, but Sammy couldn't remember ever seeing any lock on it except a button in the knob.

So he climbed to the top of the barricade and started breaking it down, one box at a time. It was like moving a mountain, but he would not be daunted. He worked steadily— and quietly, lest Aunt Nastina hear him through the floor.

Some of the cases were light, others heavy, but all could be muscled out of the way. He restacked them wherever he found space, and the once-tidy storeroom was soon choked with stock and swirling with years of settled dust. Grimy sweat dripped from Sammy's brow, and his back and arms grew stiffer with each load.

Gradually, more and more of the door came into view. And on uncovering the knob, Sammy was encouraged to see there was indeed only a button lock. He took a deep breath and dug in with renewed vigor. But after removing a few more cases, he spotted something that took away all hope: an iron bar padlocked across the width of the door.

"Oh, no," he said, on the verge of tears once more. He sat down on what remained of the barricade. "It's all been for nothing," he grieved aloud. "All for nothing."

And again the clocks struck, ten times each.

Sammy cried out sadly for his brother. "Cosmo..." He listened for an answer and then called again, "Cosmo! Why can't you hear me? Why can't you come?"

But nobody answered. Nobody came.

Hunched over, chin on his chest, Sammy started to cool off. His clothes remained damp with sweat, however, and he soon felt chilled. He sneezed once, twice, and then realized he was sitting in a draft.

"Hmmm..." he thought, getting up and walking back toward the other door. Then he spotted it—the air vent under the steps, the one Cosmo had seeped through.

"That's it!" he exclaimed, and crouched down to investigate. The hole definitely looked big enough to squeeze through. He pressed his nose to the metal grate and inhaled the briny aroma of freedom. He could make out a section of pipe running by, but otherwise it was like staring into an inkwell.

Sammy tugged on the grate and then noticed it was screwed to the floor. So he went and rifled the desk drawers for a screwdriver. He couldn't find one, but instead of panicking he tried using paper clips. They sometimes bent or slipped out of the grooves, but worked surprisingly well nonetheless.

Finally, when all the screws were out, Sammy pulled up the grate and lowered himself feet-first into the darkness. He swung his legs until he located the pipe. Then he dropped down to it, knocking off one of his tennis shoes in the process. Its splash reminded him of the fate that awaited should he fall.

Carefully now, he shinnied to a crossbeam and then paused to find his bearings. He could barely see the beam he clung to, let alone the labyrinth of timbers that lay beyond. Yet the far edges of the wharf were defined by colorful squiggles of light reflected in the water. Relying on instinct, Sammy proceeded to feel his way toward Jenko's studio.

He inched ahead slowly, crawling mostly on his hands and knees, since the planks seemed narrower and more slippery than in daytime. They were indeed damp, and his bare sock got stretched and soggy right away. But that didn't bother him as much as the cobwebs he kept running into. He couldn't stand their creepy tickling against his face.

Below, the sea swished around the pilings as though it were giggling at his misfortune. And the wharf itself could be heard groaning under the stress of time and tide. Boards creaked, chains clinked, and pipes dripped all around him.

But Sammy crawled on. He lost his way only once, when he took a dead-end route by accident and had to backtrack to another row of pilings. He knew he was on course again when he heard piano music and the stomp-and-shuffle of dancing through the floor above. These were the sounds of the Halloween party at Angelo's, which was right next door to Jenko's.

Sammy hurried now across the familiar catwalks under the studio. But as he neared the lighted area at the edge he caught a whiff of an unusual stink. The air fast became so putrid he had to stop for gagging. Then he spotted the source of the odor on a girder just overhead.

There sat the two pigeon eggs he had seen before. Only they were now cracked open. White bits of shell were scattered among the dark nest of twigs and straw. Clotted inside the two largest half-shells was a rotting yellow goo that had once been life.

Sammy was trying to make sense of it all when he heard the dry rasping of paws through straw. All of a sudden, a huge gray rat hunkered into the light at the front of the girder. It had obviously just broken into the rotten eggs, for its pointy snout was smeared with their goo.

The rat looked around suspiciously with black, beady eyes. Its head jerked in all directions. Sammy was squatting perfectly still, his back pressed against the piling, when the rodent spied him. It bared its long yellow tusks and let out a shrill hiss.

The hairs on Sammy's neck bristled and he felt a chill run down the backs of his arms. He was petrified with terror, but had enough presense of mind to arm himself. He reached down and took off his remaining tennis shoe.

The rat reared on its hind legs, exposing a belly heaving with panic. It hissed again and then pounced on Sammy with jaws wide. Sammy covered his head with one arm and lashed out blindly with the shoe in the other. He caught the rat in midair, but it held onto the sneaker and dragged his arm downward. He dropped the shoe, but the rat now clung to the sleeve of his sweatshirt. Sammy felt its claws breaking the skin and he shook his arm hysterically. At last his sleeve ripped and the rat fell groping and squealing into the inky sea.

Sammy's heart thumped in his chest. "I killed it," he panted. "I killed it!" But the relief of victory was shortlived, for a second later he saw the rat surface and begin swimming into the darkness toward another piling.

Sammy stood up and rushed to the wharf's edge. He came out under the wheeled ramp, where he saw his two partners. Jenko was sitting at the bottom of the ramp fumbling nervously with his alarm clock. He had on a bulky gray sweater and a red beret. Cosmo was pacing the dock back and forth in his white tuxedo. They seemed unaware of each other's presence.

"Hey, you guys, I'm here," Sammy shouted.

Jenko, in his surprise, threw up the clock, but luckily it landed in his lap. "Where've you been," he hollered. "I'd almost given up on you."

"It's about time!" Cosmo yelled.

"What time is it?" asked Sammy, jumping down to the dock beside his brother.

Jenko felt the hands of the clock. "It's eleven-fifteen," he said.

"We'll never make it now," moaned Cosmo.

Sammy glanced at his skiff and then looked up and saw that the moon was still clouded over. "We've got to try," he said.

"What did you say?" asked Jenko.

"I was talking to Coz," said Sammy.

"Oh," replied Jenko, as if he had forgotten why they were even there.

Sammy hurried over to him. "Come on, let's go," he said. Sammy led him toward the skif, but in their hurry Jenko nearly tripped over the old coffee can.

"Careful now," warned Jenko.

Sammy knelt down at the edge and pulled the skiff against the dock. Jenko climbed in without any trouble. The *Moonseeker* sank low under his great weight, but her gunnels remained a good eight inches above the waterline.

"Now you," said Sammy, turning to Cosmo.

Cosmo hopped in, the tails of his coat flaring out behind him. But when he landed, the boat didn't even dip.

Sammy climbed in himself now and was untying the line when Jenko said, "How'd this water get in here?"

"What water?" asked Sammy. But on looking back he saw

the puddle in the stern. "I don't know," he answered. "It wasn't here this afternoon. Maybe some of the fog melted in."

"Impossible," said Jenko. "I don't think we ought to risk it tonight. Something's the matter here."

"Tonight's the only night!" shouted Cosmo.

"Tonight's the only night," repeated Sammy.

"Well . . . at least get something to bail it out," said Jenko. "I don't want this 'melted fog' sloshing around my ankles the whole time."

Sammy climbed back out of the boat and grabbed the coffee can. Returning to the dock's edge, he saw the skiff had drifted a few feet away.

"Come on," hollered Cosmo. "Jump!"

Sammy, poised at the brink, leaped into the darkness. He landed just behind the center thwart and fell into Jenko's lap. The can clanked against the bottom boards.

"Okay, right yourself now," said Jenko. "And hand me the queen's oars."

Sammy pulled the oars out from under the thwarts and set them into place. As Jenko started rowing, Sammy started bailing.

CHAPTER THIRTEEN
Maiden Voyage

JENKO ROWED WITH DEEP, strong strokes that propelled the skiff steadily across the harbor. The white hulls of moored fishing boats loomed on all sides. Sammy, standing watch in the bow with Cosmo, directed Jenko through the fleet.

"A little to the port side," said Sammy.

"Right," said Jenko.

"No, left!" hollered Sammy. "Port is left!"

"Right. I mean aye-aye," said Jenko as he angled safely to the left.

Sammy turned and gave him a dirty look, but Jenko rowed on oblivious to it. He rocked forward and back as he worked the oars, forward and back in a smooth, rhythmic motion that sent teasing splashes up at Sammy or created shiny little whirlpools that died out just as quickly as they were born.

Sammy glanced back now at the wharf, which he had never seen before from the water. It looked unusually small and spindly, almost toylike, and it appeared to shrink the farther out Jenko rowed. Yet its amber street lamps and neon bar signs shone brightly in the darkness, as did those in town and along Cannery Row. Even the hills behind Monterey were bejeweled with house lights, and their reflections shot across the bay in shimmering streaks of liquid color.

"Squinny your peepers!" snapped Cosmo. "Purse Seiner aft the starboard beam!"

Sammy turned and saw a huge sardine boat just ahead. "Purse Seiner aft the starboard beam!" he echoed. Jenko maneuvered to the left, but glided by so close to the boat that his oar scraped its side.

"Good job," said Sammy. "Straight as she goes."

Jenko yelled over his shoulder, "Keep a sharp look-out! If I'm your arms, you're my eyes. We've got to work together."

"Aye-aye," said Sammy.

They were passing the cement breakwater now, where a blinking red warning light illuminated a congress of sea lions in heated debate. "Ark-Ark-Ark-Ark," they cried, each interrupting the other without so much as a "pardon me." One must have gotten disgusted with the argument, for it crawled clumsily over its colleagues and dove into the water.

Sounds seemed to grow sharper and carry for miles as the *Moonseeker* moved out onto the onyx bay. Sammy could hear waves tumbling onto the shore and an occasional blast from the foghorn on China Point. He leaned over the side and splashed his face with seawater. It made him feel fresh and alive.

"Man the torpedos, full speed ahead!" shouted Cosmo.

"What torpedoes?" asked Sammy.

Cosmo shrugged. "I don't know. It's just something I always wanted to say."

Sammy nodded and they both stared at the dark horizon.

"You gonna miss it here?" asked Sammy.

"Probably, although I never heard of a homesick ghost. What about you? You gonna miss me?"

"I already do."

"You'll be okay, though. You got lots of people around here to love and learn from. That's all that matters, you know."

"But I won't be able to talk to you anymore."

"Sure you will. Anytime you want. I'll always be listening. It's one of the powers we ghosts have; kind of like short-wave."

"Well then how come you didn't hear me when I was locked in the storeroom? I called you twice."

"I did hear you."

"Then why didn't you answer?"

"Who do you think reminded you about that vent?"

"You?"

Cosmo smiled smugly.

"Well, I guess short-wave is better than no-wave," said Sammy. "But won't we ever see each other again?"

"Sure," said Cosmo, "when it's your turn to visit me."

"Aren't you even a little scared?" asked Sammy. "What if it's no fun where you're going?"

"Oh, it'll be great, Sammy. It's a whole 'nother world to explore. And we have people out there too, remember."

"I know."

"I'll tell them hi for you when I see 'em."

"Thanks," said Sammy.

Jenko looked back. "What are you guys talking about now?"

"Just stuff," said Sammy. "What time is it?"

Jenko put up one oar and pulled the clock out of his coat pocket. "Here," he said, handing it to Sammy, "keep it dry."

The moon still hadn't shown itself, but Sammy could read the clock by its light. It said eleven-thirty-six. "Can't we go any faster?" he asked.

"How much seahorsepower do you think I got in these arms?" said Jenko. "Tell you what, climb in the stern. We may move a little faster that way."

Sammy tucked the clock in his sweatshirt and climbed carefully over Jenko. Once seated, he noticed that Jenko's bearded face was dripping with sweat. But the old able-bodied seaman hadn't slackened his pace one bit. It was a race against time—a race-in-reverse, in fact—and he put his back into every stroke.

Sammy suddenly became aware of his cold, wet feet. He looked down at the puddle that had formed since he last bailed. He peeled off his sopping socks and threw them overboard. Then he found the can and started bailing again.

"Are we still taking in water?" asked Jenko.

"Just a little," said Sammy.

"Where's it coming in from?"

"I don't know. I think this one corner here."

"I thought you sealed the transom up good?"

"I did, but maybe the nails pulled out when she fell off the sawhorses this afternoon."

"Nails? You used nails? I told you to use screws!"

"I know. I didn't think it would make any difference."

"That does it. We're turning back."

"Don't let him, Sammy!" exclaimed Cosmo from the bow.

"You can't," said Sammy. "It's just leaking a little. I can keep it bailed out."

"This is crazy!" yelled Jenko. "We're liable to drown out here!"

"I won't let you," said Cosmo.

"Cosmo says he won't let us," pleaded Sammy. "Look, there's the bell buoy. We're halfway there."

"Ah, for cryin' out loud," hollered Jenko. "If I don't live to regret this night, I'll . . . I'll follow Cosmo and ring his neck. And you can tell him I said so!"

Cosmo grinned.

"He heard you," said Sammy.

Old Gao, sitting on a rock on China Point, also heard Jenko's shouts as they carried over the calm sea. At first he thought they were the ghostly cries of his countrymen who had suffered through the Chinatown fire almost fifty years ago. But then he saw the boat bobbing in the moonlight a half mile off shore.

Gao stood up and cupped his ear. He heard two voices now. They were certainly agitated, but the only words he could make out were "crazy" and "drown out here." Gao called out, "Hey, you in the boat. You okay?"

The answer was a guttural BAAAAAH! from the foghorn behind him. Gao turned and snarled at the ugly concrete bunker mounted with loudspeakers. Looking back out to sea, he saw that the boat was heading toward the treacherous waters over the Monterey Trench.

Who could be out there this time of night? he wondered. And what were they doing? They weren't fishing. Then he remembered Sammy and Jenko's plan for a so-called bay cruise. He sucked air and shook his head with concern. "Stupid guys," he muttered.

A lifetime in Monterey had taught Gao to mind his own business. Yet he felt responsible for Sammy in a way he hadn't felt about anyone in years, not since he cursed the bay. What if they're in trouble, he asked himself. What if something bad happens to them? Gao fretted over what to do, but then made up his mind to at least find out if it was them out there. He took off at a fast trot down the railroad tracks toward the wharf.

Gao made good time, as the wooden ties laid by his forefathers were spaced perfectly to match his quick little steps. On reaching the wharf, he went straight to Aunt Nastina's flat and knocked on the door. The porch light flicked on and the door opened as wide as its chain would allow. Aunt Nastina stuck her face in the crack. She was in her bathrobe and wore no make-up.

"Go away," she said. "I don't believe in trick-or-treat."

"It's Sammy," said Gao, still breathing hard. "I think he's in trouble out on the bay."

Aunt Nastina now recognized Gao. "I'll thank you not to go bothering people at this hour," she replied. "I know exactly where my nephew is and it's not out on the bay."

"But I think I heard them—him and Jenko. And they told me they going out tonight."

"Yes, I know all about their lunatic scheme. I even know you had a hand in it, giving Sammy money to repair that wreck. I don't appreciate it one bit."

"Ai-yaaa!" said Gao. "You wasting time. They may be caught in a current and can't get back in."

Aunt Nastina's face showed the strain of appearing unworried. "I'll prove it," she said. "Follow me."

She grabbed her keys and threw off the chain, and they hurried around to the shop's entrance. She let Gao and herself in and then proceeded to the storeroom. "I had to do this for his own good," she explained along the way. On reaching the door, she called through it, "Sammy, I'm here. It's time to go up to bed." When there was no answer, she assured Gao, "He must have fallen asleep already."

Aunt Nastina unlocked the door and turned on the storeroom light. She saw the jumble of boxes and knew at once that something was terribly wrong.

"Sammy, I know you're in here," she persisted in a wavering tone that told she knew nothing of the sort.

Gao walked down the steps to look behind some of the stacked cases. He then spotted the open vent. "There," he said. "He got out there. He's on the bay all right."

The clocks in the gift shop suddenly tolled out the first of four dozen dreadful knells declaring the midnight hour.

Aunt Nastina staggered down the steps and grabbed the

lapels of Gao's coat. "You've got to do something," she cried over the din. "He's all I have."

Gao patted her hands. "Come with me."

At that very moment, about a mile off shore, Sammy stood up in the skiff waving Jenko's alarm clock over his head. "Now!" he yelled. "We have to do it now!"

"I don't think we're over the trench yet," said Cosmo.

"But it's time," said Sammy. "It's straight-up twelve!"

Jenko pulled in both oars and massaged his sore arms. The last quarter-mile had been hard slogging. So much water had leaked in the skiff that it rowed like a loaded barge. Jenko flexed his stiff back. "Now find me the can," he ordered. "Give me the can."

As Sammy obeyed, Cosmo peeled off his tuxedo jacket. "Here goes nothing," he said. He climbed onto the edge of the bow, looked up at the veiled moon, and sang out:

> *"Oogli-kaboon,*
> *Up to the moon.*
> *Oogli-kalide,*
> *Rise with the tide . . . "*

Then he dove into the water and disappeared into its blackness. Sammy gripped the gunnels nervously as he watched for his brother to reappear. Cosmo broke to the surface a moment later and started doing the back stroke as he repeated the rhyme:

> *"Oogli-kaboon,*
> *Up to the moon.*
> *Oogli-kalide,*
> *Rise with the tide . . . "*

But nothing happened.

"What's wrong?" hollered Sammy.

"We're sinking!" said Jenko. "Help me."

"I don't know," cried Cosmo. "It's not working."

"Keep trying!" screamed Sammy.

"Keep bailing!" yelled Jenko.

Back on the wharf, outside Angelo's bar, two candle-brained jack-o'-lanterns glowed in the night. The smell of singed pumpkin wafted through the open door, where the Halloween party was in full swing. Music was playing, people were dancing, and a fire was blazing in the fireplace.

Everyone had on a costume except Angelo, who was tending bar in his white apron and bow tie. As he wiped out an ashtray, he checked his watch for the umpteenth time that hour. His eyes bugged, and he began banging the ashtray on the bar and shouting, "Cut the music! Cut the music! It's almost midnight."

Angelo's brother was at the piano wearing a white sheet, impersonating the now notorious ghost of Fisherman's Wharf. Benny was in his patriot's costume, keeping time on a snare drum. Both stopped playing as Angelo led a mass countdown.

"Five—four—three—two—one—HAPPY HALLOWEEN!"

At the stroke of midnight the revelers cheered and threw off their masks. Sergeant Abner was revealed as the one in the gorilla suit. Babe was obviously the Viking, with his horned helmet and sword. Ratzo was wrapped in the mummy rags. And his wife was gowned like a fairy princess with a tin foil wand. The actresses were here too. The queen, now a vampire, had fangs and a black cape. And the Indian, now a pirate, wore an eye-patch and penciled mustache. Everyone laughed and pointed, and as the music started up again they all resumed dancing.

Into this mad scene rushed Gao and Nastina. They dashed past the flickering jack-o'-lanterns, pushed across the crowded dance floor, and shouldered up to the bar. A drunken bull fighter sitting on a barrel looked up at them and said, "Great costumes!" Old Gao growled at the guy and then waved Angelo over.

"What'll it be?" said Angelo.

"No drink," said Gao. "We need help for Sammy and Jenko." He pointed toward the bay. "They in trouble out on the water!"

"What kind of trouble?" asked Angelo.

"I don't know," said Gao, "but I heard them yelling off China Point. Maybe they caught in a current, or even sinking."

"I hope not," said Angelo. "There are sharks out there."

"Don't even talk that way!" cried Aunt Nastina.

"Sorry, sorry," said Angelo. He looked around until he spotted the gorilla dancing with Babe. "Abner! Abner, come over here," he called.

Abner, now wearing the Viking helmet, waltzed Babe off the dance floor. Although he was out of uniform, the sergeant's professional instincts were on duty. He suspected something was amiss the moment he saw Gao and Nastina. "What's the problem?" he asked.

"Jenko and Sammy are out on the bay," explained Angelo. "Old Gao heard them yelling off China Point. They're probably being swept out over the trench. Or worse."

Abner looked shocked at Aunt Nastina. "You mean he actually went through with it?"

"Yes, Mr. Psychology, he actually went through with it," she answered. "Thanks to you!"

"Wait a minute, Agnestina. I never said . . . "

Benny saw them arguing from across the room and stopped

playing. So did Angelo's brother. Without the music, everyone now noticed the commotion at the bar and huddled around, demanding to know what was going on.

"There's nothing to worry about," announced Sergeant Abner. "Little Sammy is out on the bay with Jenko. That's all. We're deciding on a course of action."

"Oh, my God!" gasped Ratzo's wife, and she went over to embrace Nastina.

"Call the Coast Guard!" shouted the vampire.

"Notify the Navy!" urged the pirate.

"Hold on a second," said Abner. "I'm in charge here. Angelo, call the Coast Guard. Babe, notify the Navy."

"No time," said Gao. "Isn't there a fisherman here, some-one with a boat?"

"I got the *Pippina Louise,*" said Babe. "She's tied up behind Ratzo's market."

"Okay, then take off," said Abner. "Sweep past the point and head toward the trench."

Babe grabbed the Viking helmet off Abner and put it back on his own head. "I'm on my way," he said he-roically. Then he added, "Ratzo, I could use a second mate."

"I'm right behind you," said Ratzo.

"I'll come," offered the pirate.

"Me too," said the vampire.

"No, no," said Babe. "The two of us are enough. What we all might need, though, is a light on the point. Why don't you go build a bonfire out there? It'll help give us and the boy some bearings."

"Good idea," said Abner.

As everyone headed for the door, Angelo called out, "Hey, don't everybody go. The party's not over."

But everybody did go, including his brother and Benny,

who carried off the jack-o'-lanterns to help guide the group down the railroad tracks.

Angelo, finding himself alone, took off his apron, rolled it up, and threw it under the bar. "Wait up," he hollered. "No use missing all the action on account of a little business."

CHAPTER FOURTEEN
Discovery

THE *MOONSEEKER* WAS FAST becoming swamped. Nearly a foot of frigid bay water had leaked in through the transom. Jenko bailed and bailed, but the water kept rising. Sammy was still too preoccupied with his brother's plight to be aware of his own danger. He watched anxiously as Cosmo swam back and forth off the bow.

"It's too late," yelled Cosmo.

"No, one more time," urged Sammy.

"All right," said Cosmo, "but you say it too. As he started the rhyme, Sammy joined in:

> *"Oogli-kaboon,*
> *Up to the moon.*
> *Oogli-kalide,*
> *Rise with the tide . . . "*

Their fervent voices rose skyward, but that was all.

"It's no use," said Cosmo, and he began swimming back to the skiff. On reaching it, he held onto the knotted rope hanging over the bow. He gazed pathetically up at Sammy, as if all his hopes had been dashed against a shoal and the bleakest of futures was staring him in the face.

"Why didn't it work?" cried Sammy.

"I don't know," said Cosmo. "Maybe it's too late. Or maybe we're not out far enough. Either way, I'm stuck." He wiped away the seawater dripping into his eyes.

"That can't be!" railed Sammy. "I did everything you said."

"I know," said Cosmo, "You tried your best. We all did."

"Then why won't you rise? It's not fair!" And Sammy heaved the clock at the cowardly moon still hiding above the fog.

"It's okay," said Cosmo. "There are worse things than being a wharf spook. And we can always try again in nineteen years."

"No," screamed Sammy. "You've got to go now!"

Jenko yelled, "What's the matter? Why aren't you bailing?"

"It didn't work," cried Sammy. "He didn't rise."

"Forget about that," said Jenko. "We're in big trouble here."

Sammy now noticed the oars drifting away from the skiff. He reached for the nearest one and all the water in the boat sloshed that way, sweeping him over the side.

"Whoa now!" hollered Jenko as he rode out the surge. "What happened? Where are you?"

Sammy surfaced spewing out seawater. He floundered noisily until he saw Cosmo and the *Moonseeker.* He splashed back to the boat and clung to her side like a starfish to a piling. Jenko heard him panting and pulled him back in.

"What are you trying to do," he said, "capsize us?"

Sammy didn't answer. The cold plunge had shocked him into realizing that they could easily drown before the night was over. He looked at the sparkling lights on shore, which now seemed farther away than the stars. Angrily, he turned toward Cosmo.

"I never should have listened to you," he yelled. "This was a stupid idea to begin with. Whoever heard of riding up a moonbeam? You should have just whispered into some kid's ear and left like normal."

"I tried," said Cosmo.

"You did?" said Sammy.

Cosmo just gazed sadly at his brother.

"You mean me?" asked Sammy. He paused and then said, "Of course you do. Why wouldn't I count? You've given me all kinds of new ideas."

"Like what?" questioned Cosmo.

"Like about fixing up this old skiff, and listening, you know, to the tide or to what old Gao knows, and not hating guys like Red. All that stuff. Why doesn't that count?"

Cosmo smiled and looked up. The high ceiling of fog began to shift and break up into wispy patches. The sky lightened and then the moon itself emerged in all its overflowing brilliance. Rays streaked down like search lights, all of them pointed at Cosmo. His hair stood on end and the water in it started dripping upwards and throwing off colorful sparks. Slowly, very slowly, Cosmo began sliding head-first up the moonbeam.

"It only counts if you know it counts," he crowed, six feet over the ocean.

"Look!" said Sammy.

"What? What do you see?" asked Jenko worriedly.

"He's rising!"

"At last!"

"He's all lit up," continued Sammy, "and spouting sparks like a . . . like a little volcano."

"Holy Stromboli!" exclaimed Jenko.

Cosmo, now at least a hundred feet up, shouted, "So long, Sammy. And thanks for everything. You're the best brother there could ever beeeeee. . . . "

Cosmo's voice trailed off as he slid toward the moon. Up, up, up he rose, higher and higher, until he was completely absorbed into its brightness.

"So long," whispered Sammy.

As he watched, a white gull-shaped blur rose out of the dark fog, streaked black across the pale moon, and disappeared again into the far side of the sky.

"Is he gone?" asked Jenko. "Did the moonbeam take him?"

"No," said Sammy. "He took the moonbeam."

Jenko didn't have time to reflect on the difference. The *Moonseeker's* gunnels now floated level with the waterline and the sea was as much inside as out. "Good, good. We're still all right," he babbled nervously. "No need to panic."

Sammy lowered his gaze and considered the foundering skiff. "Are we gonna just hang on till morning?" he asked.

"No, it's too cold," said Jenko, "we'll have to swim for it."

"Oh," said Sammy. But after thinking a while he added, "But there are sharks out here. I know, I've seen Babe bring them in."

"Ah, those are just basking sharks; they're not man-eaters."

"They might be boy-eaters."

"No, you don't have to worry."

Sammy looked toward shore, but couldn't find it. The fog had settled low, blanketing the hillside lights.

"It's a long way back," said Sammy. I don't know if I can swim that far."

"Lucky for you I was a champion breast stroker in my younger days," replied Jenko. "I can tow you."

Sammy eyed him skeptically and asked, "What weren't you in your younger days?"

"Hey, I've got the medals to prove it," boasted Jenko. "Or at least I had them. Anyway, you'll see." He removed his sweater and beret and then reached down to pull off his soggy sneakers.

"But what about the *Moonseeker?*" asked Sammy. "We can't just abandon her."

"We've got to," said Jenko. And to ease the boy's fears he sang a verse from the old chantey:

> *"The rats have gone and we the crew*
> *Must leave her, Sammy, leave her.*
> *It's time, by God, that we went too.*
> *It's time for us to leave her."*

"Okay," said Sammy.

Jenko slipped over the side and Sammy put his arms around his neck. "Here we go," said Jenko as he pushed off the skiff. They glided smoothly through the black, glassy sea. Jenko hadn't lost his winning form and Sammy was able to ride him like a porpoise. The former champion came up for air every other stroke, but Sammy kept his head above water at all times.

After a while he asked, "Are we going the right way? I can't see land anymore."

"I think so," said Jenko. "Listen for the fog horn." In a minute the familiar *BAAAAAH!* sounded off to their left. They corrected their course and continued on.

The pace was slow and easy, but even so the chill began to take its toll. Jenko's arms grew heavy as anchors and cramps started stabbing him in the side. He had to stop several times to float on his back and rest.

Sammy, too, was stiff with fatigue and woozy from all the bobbing. He couldn't tell if they were making headway or struggling in vain against a current. And sometimes he didn't even care. He wished he could just close his eyes and go with the gentle rocking. His fear of the deep, however, kept him alert. He felt that at any moment a shark would zoom up from below and bite him in half, or an octopus would wrap a tentacle around his foot and pull him down.

"I've got to rest, Sammy," Jenko said once more. He took Sammy's hand and they both floated on their backs. "I guess I'm not in the shape I thought I was," he admitted. "I don't know if I can go on."

"Relax," said Sammy. "I'll tow *you* if I have to."

Sammy rolled over and tried to kick higher out of the water to look for the shore. But the fog had socked in the entire bay and he couldn't see more than twenty yards in any direction.

"What's that?" he said, spying something in the water.

"What's what?" asked Jenko.

"That thing over there. It's sticking up like a fin, a shark's fin. Oh, Jenko, don't let it get us!"

"Keep still. Maybe it'll go away."

"It's not. It's getting closer."

"Quiet. And don't splash."

Sammy watched in horror as the perceived predator floated ever closer. It moved slowly, cautiously, as if unsure of the nature of its prey. Sammy now began to question his own eyes. "Wait a minute," he said. "I don't think it is a shark. It looks more like a log, with a branch sticking up."

"Are you sure?" asked Jenko, hopefully. "Are you sure?"

"I'm gonna find out," said Sammy. He let go of Jenko's hand and swam toward the dark object.

"Don't! Come back!" yelled Jenko.

But Sammy kept going, determined to punch it in the nose even if it was just a basker. When he reached it, however, he discovered that it wasn't a shark after all, but some kind of piling. "We're saved," he yelled and pushed it back to Jenko.

"I don't believe it," said Jenko as he clung exhausted to the log. "It's a miracle!" He rested his cheek against the wet wood and rubbed it lovingly as he caught his breath. Suddenly he lifted his head and ran his hand down the length of the log. A huge smile appeared on his face. "Guess what?" he said. "This isn't just any old stump; it's my Columbus!"

"No!" said Sammy in disbelief. He looked down and found himself staring Cosmo in the eye. "You're right, it is him. And that's no branch pointing up, it's his arm!"

"Hey, hey," said Jenko. "What do you think of that?"

"I told you he wouldn't let us drown," said Sammy.

They straddled the sculpture and started paddling it in like a surfboard, Sammy in front and Jenko in back. Soon they heard waves breaking against rocks and knew they had reached China Point. Sammy then saw a light flickering on the beach and shadowy figures milling around it.

"There's a fire," he said. "Some hobos must have built a bonfire."

"Great!" said Jenko. "But what's that behind us?"

Sammy heard it now, too; it was the hum of a diesel engine. He glanced back and saw a beautiful white-hulled fishing boat with all her running lights on, idling just outside the rocks. He recognized Babe and Ratzo steering from atop the cabin and he waved to them.

"It's the *Pippina Louise*," said Sammy. "Babe must be fishing squid already."

"Must be," said Jenko.

Sammy looked up again at the moon, which glowed gloriously through the patches of fog. He knew that Cosmo was now a part of its glow, a presence to be felt forever, whether seen or not.

Jenko's Epilogue

... IT WASN'T LONG before the little waves tossed us ashore at China Point. Everyone on the beach rushed down and dragged us back to the fire, where we exchanged hugs all around. It was the warmest welcome I've had to this day.

But of course Abner and Nastina and the others soon felt sufficiently relieved to bawl us out for the folly of our ways. Sammy had to assure them that yes, Cosmo had left for good. And I had to promise that no, I'd never do anything so foolish again.

Then we all headed back to the wharf. We must have made a marvelous sight marching down the tracks. Sammy led the procession riding atop old Gao's shoulders. Nastina and I followed behind arm-in-arm. And then came all the others, with Benny, Abner and the actresses carrying Columbus.

Later on, all the folks on the wharf got together and dedicated the statue on a bluff overlooking the bay. I'm proud to say it's still there today, pointing toward the horizon.

So there you have it, the whole story of the ghost of Fisherman's Wharf. I told you I'd finish before the full moon faded and dawn pinkened on the eastern sky.

There *is* one thing I failed to mention, though. Shortly after I got up and started this story, I noticed that I, like Cosmo, had left my body behind. What a sight to greet me after all these years in the dark! Look, it's lying there in my bed, cold as that marble bust in the corner.

Heh, heh. But don't worry about me. I expect I'll soon see wonders and colors never imagined by any earth-moored artist. Yes, having told you this tale—whispered it into your ear, so to speak—I, too, am free to rise with the tide.